Invasion of the Baby Daddy

By

Dr. John Bell

Invasion of the Baby Daddy

By

Dr. John Bell

www.jamarhouse.com

Dr. Ron Davis, Editor

CONTENTS

1: Single man looking for a woman   7

2: How I met my wife   17

3: What expecting means to a relationship   27

4: Everyone, yet no one really knows   38

5: How the law can give a "baby daddy" control   43

over a marriage

6: When baby daddies are around like a phantom   55

7: When marriage is tested what do you do?   64

8: The Joseph Syndrome: Getting away from the unexpected   89

9: How we survived a tragedy   114

10: When a Miracle happens and life begins   119

11: Afterthoughts   124

12: 10 Pearls of Wisdom if marrying a man/woman with a child.   125

ACKNOWLEDGEMENTS

I would first like to thank my wife and family for all of their support and ever-giving love to me. I would also like to thank God for blessing me to find someone to give me love when I first believed that love could never be found. I want to express my gratitude to all of my colleagues that have been in my life from the very beginning of my career. I dedicate this book to all my children, especially the unborn and my first born child, Amber. Also, to the generations to come, I pray they will learn from the wisdom of this book. May God bless the reader of this work and allow the passion of life to fill their heart with knowledge.

To my Mother, who has been a great supporter of my efforts for all of my life, I say thank you for being there for me. I could not have been blessed with a better person to usher me into the world. You are indeed a jewel without price, and I am humbled to call you mom. To all of my immediate family and distant relatives, I also say, "Thank you for all of your support." Truly my life has been blessed by your presence. To everyone I have ever known in the past, present or, perhaps, the future. My life has been and will be enriched by your presence and season of time in it. It is evident that no one enters our atmosphere without a reason. Life has allowed all things to evolve and manifest itself for our life's greater purpose. That goal and purpose is for all people to be better with everyone who has ever affected our lives. It is truly how we all participate in the circle of life and learn from each other in our daily lives. It gives me the opportunity to thank all the people I have ever met and shared a part of my life with. I wish you all nothing but peace, happiness and satisfaction. May your journey be even better today, after sharing your world with me.

This book was written to inform and enlighten all who read it of the power of the human spirit and how true determination and will of life can overcome the greatest of challenges that can occur in marriages.

1
<u>Single man looking for a woman</u>

As once a single man, I often pondered what life would hold in store for me. I never really knew how to approach the reality of looking for a woman to marry. I often figured it would happen like it does in the movies. You know how the guy meets this woman, and they have a few dates. During the courtship, the man would say the greatest lines and as a result, the woman would be swept off her feet. The rest is history. No drama or challenges, the end.

We all know that we do not live in that movie, well most of us anyway. Love, at first sight, is truly a great misconception (or even second or third for that matter). With maturity and experience as both a Father and Husband, I never expected to meet a woman, who already had a child, to be my wife. Furthermore, my expectation was that I would meet someone on my level; like a physician or lawyer—someone who was equally yoked or of my intellectual stature.

Once you have wrestled with the challenges of being a young man; you learn how to become a better one. Your selection of women evolves from what you want, to what you need.

Selfishness in relationships is commonplace to many men. This characteristic is practically encoded in our DNA. As we are raised to be gladiators, we compete for things, such as: family pride, home turf and always for young love or infatuation. This selfishness is also the core of how most men are defined in their relationships with women. The selfishness quotient of a man translates into how he treats himself and the woman to whom he will make a life commitment.

"Dr. Mark Sand, you selfish bastard!" I said this, while gazing into a mirror, reflecting on my past.

I deserved to have any woman that I wanted. Most guys my age, (i.e., young, twenty-something) think that they know everything about the world. So did I. Choosing a woman was supposed to be my privilege. Like most men, I was completely off base with my chauvinistic delusions of grandeur. My mentality was that women should cater to men and show the man consistent affection.

This distorted type of thinking limits the emotional health of a

7

man by polluting his contribution to a relationship. It was this paradox of selfishness that challenged my encounters with the opposite sex. I was not without competition, as most women that I met, possessed their own agendas of what they wanted from men. They were, at times, delusional themselves. When two selfish people meet each other, lonely and desperate for affection and broken from past experiences, the natural outcome is always disaster.

Although I can not speak for all women, the ones who I have encountered have been either more than, or just as selfish as me. Do not get me wrong, my share of past experiences have promoted an emotional instability that makes me look like a misogynist. This characteristic can mostly be recognized in situations where a young man is raised by a single woman with little or no male exposure to emulate. Matters are made worse by living in highly impoverished conditions. Some ask, how can this make young men selfish? The answer to that question was quite easy for me. I was bitter when I had to live in "the hood." I developed a hatred for men, who were not man enough to care for my mother, my siblings and me. Growing up, witnessing crime and broken dreams, made the most vulnerable of male children (females too) bitter. Nonetheless, I can only speak of my experiences. There were times that I felt that women caused men to leave home. Out of my own foolishness, I blamed my mother for not being wise or educated enough to know how to choose a good father for me.

So when you see "the experts" talk about where selfishness and bitterness comes from, in our black, disenfranchised children, know that it begins early and manifests itself through shared-lived experiences. My early bout with selfishness has somewhat evolved. This comes as a result of my resilient nature, due to my depravity in dealing with issues, such as: having no father or stable economic existence. I felt that if I ever had a chance to change my situation, I would make up for lost time.

This attitude can be identified by most young men, who are reared in similar situations. As my attitude manifested its ugliness, during the initial phase of my dating life, it remained the mental undercurrent for most of my young, adult life. Eventually, it led to my mentality-changing fear of becoming a "baby daddy."

I was about 19 years-old when I joined the U.S. Navy. I was stationed on the USS Arkansas CGN-41, a guided missile cruiser, out of Alameda, California. I was so glad to get out of "the hood" of Mt. Morris, Michigan and experience freedom. The Navy allowed me to see what the "other half" of the world looked like. I felt like a bird out of a cage, especially since I was now earning my own money. I never imagined that I would be living in San Francisco, enjoying warm weather and beautiful people, while having a roof over my head. This was not a bad way of life, considering that I had come from a life of food stamps and the humiliation of poverty and hopelessness.

I have always said, "The U.S. Navy was a great place for me, because it took me from the hood to the rest of the world and for that I am eternally grateful."

This is where I met Sheila, my first, real girlfriend. It was here that I fell in love with my whole heart. Even then, I was only interested in my own sexual gratification. I wanted her to experience this too, but you know how young studs are: We want to cum first and catch the female on the rebound. As this relationship lasted for about a year, I grew to believe that I would marry her. I was so happy that I informed my mother. As I was 19-years-old and finally coming into my own, the military took me away from her when the Gulf War broke out in 1991. We were a part of the USS Carl Vincent battle group, as we were called to duty. I was actually excited because I thought we would only be out to sea for a week or so. Well, what I thought would take a week; turned out to last about 6 months away from my first love—I was devastated. My world was caving in, and the past feelings of hopelessness and despair became familiar to me again. I wrote to Sheila daily and she wrote back for a while, until, gradually, the letters began to dwindle.

Regardless of my 19-year-old feelings of abandonment, I had to focus because we were at war and within firing distance from the enemy forces. So there I was—heartbroken, abandoned and scared to death. This consistent threat of death, coupled with my personal situation, promoted constant prayers that we would not hit a mine in enemy territory. Consequently, this was also my first real heartbreak as a grown man.

I found it impossible to not think about her, while keeping my wits focused on the fact that I was in the middle of the Gulf War. Everyday, we had to appear physically ready and be mentally focused. I remembered that I would never dare tell my shipmates what had just happened between me and Sheila. As most sailors know, you have to give the persona that you are "the man," with females in ports all over the world. More importantly, no one likes to hear sad stories in war, when everyone is scared and trying to focus on getting out alive. At times, it seemed almost impossible to endure. As we would hear tomahawk missiles flying overhead, we remained in a lockdown battle station area.

After the war, I returned home to find that my relationship had changed. My first girlfriend had joined the U.S. Naval Reserves and was going off to Virginia for training. Although my heart was still breaking, I loved her. I wanted to see her again. After two years of prayer, our paths finally crossed in Norfolk, Virginia. It was surreal to see the woman that I had both known and loved. She had a failed engagement, an aborted pregnancy and was trying to restore herself through church. A mutual friend got us back in touch with one another, and I felt like God was giving me a second chance.

When I arrived in Virginia, I gave Sheila a ring and a stuffed bear from Australia. I really thought it was our reunion, as we talked and gently kissed. Passions flowed and sex happened. It was beautiful to me, but in midst of the night, I noticed her crying and sobbing. She began to tell me about her horribly-ended engagement and an abortion she underwent.

Crying uncontrollably, wroth with emotion, she asked, "Why did you come here?"

I have to say that those words continue to haunt me to this day. My, once, girlfriend left our bed of passion and went downstairs crying and sobbing. I felt bad that I did not understand how to handle the situation. Being emotionally inexperienced and confused with her reaction, I remained in bed for what proved to be one of the longest weekends of my life. I was with a stranger, and my girlfriend was gone. Re-living this period of my life brings back painful memories; however, telling the truth is therapeutic. It also explains the hardening of my exterior shell of selfishness.

The weekend ended with us hanging on to the moment. I could tell that she was not feeling what we had anymore, and it hurt like hell to see that face-to-face. At that moment, I would have preferred to be back in war and not there, in Virginia. I could see how my life had stood still during war, while her life progressed with relationships and adult-level realities, in which I remained inexperienced. My attempts to console her were met by emotionally-driven blockades. Finally, at the airport, she told me that she wanted me to have a good life. She explained that my love for her was "unrealistic," because I was attempting to hold on to the woman that she once was.

With tears in her eyes, her last words to me were, "Don't watch me walk away."

I could not help but to watch her walk out of sight. I admit that I had tears in my eyes. What was worse was that my soul had been torn inside out. The scar that remained would, eventually, become home to many additional ones. Men usually try to 'play off' their emotions, in the midst of deep pain or heartbreak; however, truthfully, when the heartbreak is not caused by a man being a "player" or a "dog" to a woman, this type of heartbreak can be almost psychologically crippling.

Since that event, I put up all kinds of road blocks to my heart and tried not to be hurt like that again. That event resurrected my selfishness and made me want to retaliate at women, while trying to heal from my first girlfriend's infliction of pain. I did meet another girl, the following year, at a local church in California. Tonya had two, young children. One was about 7 or 8, and the other was 2. She showed me great interest and affection. Although I was not looking for a woman with children, her presence was like an antidote to an illness. Tonya became a great confidant, as we shared great times. Ironically, her baby daddy was involved with his children. As a 20-year-old, I had gone from being hurt to, now, juggling a relationship with a woman, who had children and a family-oriented baby daddy.

My new lady and I became engaged, as I left California to pursue my education at Morris College in Sumter, S.C. I was 22 at the time, and was without a good male counselor. As I analyzed Tonya's lifestyle, I discovered that she had some baby daddy issues that were too much for me. This was my first encounter of dealing with a woman, who was tied to another man. The baby daddy's persistent campaign for her was successful. Naturally, our engagement ended, and I found myself alone, again. This experience was different from Sheila's. With Tonya, I felt cheated. The commonality of both experiences showed me that women were living and enjoying their lives, while I was off either fighting a war or trying to achieve a future through education.

I have always wondered: "Why do good guys never seem to get the best looking or the young, fine girls? If I am truly a "good catch," then why do I find myself having to give that "Last guy on the floor" speech? Most important, why were these kinds of women the best that I could find? I was beginning to feel that I would have to sacrifice, the younger, finer woman, without kids; for the older, more down-to-earth woman, with children.

It became a struggle to find someone, and I looked everywhere. Some women referred to me as "too big," while some would state that I was "too nerdy." I had heard it all.

The one question that consistently remained as I dated was "How do the baby daddies seem to get all the fine women and how do they meet them?"

I would go to church and the club, every so often, to socialize and see if there were any "good women" out there who wanted a relationship that could amount to something. In many instances, I felt that I was competing with players and married men who wanted something on the side and worst of all, the casual baby daddy. I understood the *player*. They were out having fun or sex or both. Usually, players are pretty responsible and do not leave any kids behind. Most of them use condoms, so they do not lose a dollar out of their paycheck. The *married man* is simply looking for casual sex and no drama. He is also looking for companionship, when he can fit it into his every "now-and-then" schedule. Married men usually like the occasional relationship that gives them the alternative to what they have at home, but without commitment. The elusive *baby daddy* actually wants to get into a woman's head and seduce her into sacrificing her most precious inner-self to him. When a woman is vulnerable at this point, no one cares about condoms; it is all about the baby daddy's satisfaction. Whatever happens to the woman, or his seed, is what it is. None of these male prototypes are the optimal male to emulate; however, the baby daddy does the most damage by limiting the woman's selection process for a better suitor in life, based on his agenda.

The baby daddy also has a place forever in the woman's life. This could be detrimental on the children and psychologically dismantling to the woman. Generally, two or more lives are destroyed by the baby daddy's selfishness. He is most definitely not the marrying type. They just seem to add others to their list of victims as carnage. As they captivate their victim, the woman falls in love but later becomes invaded. At this time, the trap of caring for an unplanned child, whom he will often not support, has been set. Moreover, this union generally produces life-long, negative effects and regrets, in which the woman, caught in this vicious cycle, cannot economically, psychologically and often physically recover. This, ultimately, alters her future, for selecting a better mate in life.

Knowing this, I continued to mature as a man. I did not want to repeat the curse that I was born into. I also knew that I did not want to damage women, or most importantly, any potentially created children. As a result, I wore a condom at all times. I did not want any children out of wedlock. I was not perfect, but like most guys, I dated and desired sex. This was also dangerous, because while my libido assisted in the fulfillment of my carnal pleasures, I was still emotionally scared from my previous relationships.

I dated a few Physicians when I was in Cleveland, Ohio, where I attended medical school. At one point, I actually thought I was going to marry Felicia, a resident physician, but she and I had something negative in common. She proved to be just as selfish and nitpicky as I was about dating. I found her to be a brilliant physician, but emotionally bankrupt and very stubborn. I was stubborn too. Felicia did not allow me to snore or eat, at anytime. I could not be myself, as there was no pleasing her. I wanted my way too, as I would refuse to compromise on anything. I remember telling her that if we got married, that she could not hyphenate her maiden name.

Felicia was her father's only daughter and they held a close relationship. I was frustrated that I could not have my way. We

13

eventually crashed and burned, and I was badly hurt after this breakup. I really pined over our breakup because I really wanted to marry a doctor. My plans were to have a great life, with someone who was on my level. Although I was devastated, I never told her, but our break up hurt me badly.

From Cleveland, Ohio, I went to Aliquippa, Pennsylvania for my first year of residency. With all of my experiences; I had grown as a man. Again, I found myself looking for a stable relationship. I did meet another young lady who had two kids, and once again, I found myself wounded. I relentlessly pursued companionship. Linda was a beautiful woman who had been married and divorced. Naturally, her situation did not fit the baby-daddy category, but what she told me has stayed with me throughout my life. One evening, at her home, we began to casually discuss our lives. She told me that her ex-husband still attended all the family gatherings and holidays with their children. She explained that they had been married for over 10 years and had a good family relationship. I met him once, and I felt uncomfortable around the children, with him there. He did not know that I was seeing his ex-wife, as we were pretty discrete and on the down low with our intimacy. She told me that even though they were divorced, she would always love him because he gave her children. Their children also had a strong love for their father. This was very confusing and painful for me.

I recall thinking, "You can't be number one to someone who already has that spot reserved."

I was determined to not relinquish my pursuit for real love. I was also determined to beat out the baby daddies who seemed to always beat me to the best and most caring women. I was getting older now. I was alone, but not desperate. I knew that I would be a good husband, someday. I had made some bad mistakes and was trying to get on track. The baby-daddy syndrome consistently seemed to find its way to my life's front door. I was going to church quite regularly, as I needed spiritual guidance and healing. I did not have a father figure in my life, except uncles whom I rarely saw a few times a year. I had some great friends, who gave their advice. Their selection of women seemed to be better than mine.

Ironically, when a man gets to this level in life, love is not work anymore. It is simply a fantasy awaiting fulfillment through disappointment, heartache or depression. I cannot speak for all men, but for me, masturbation became a relaxation technique. Sometimes, it was a venue for me to get to sleep. Afterwards, I still had a void, in my heart, as I was empty both physically and emotionally. I was looking for the right woman. Furthermore, I was yet hopeful not to become a baby daddy. I had enough experience and advice to know that I simply did not want anymore women, who already had children. I was also determined to defeat the baby daddies who kept intercepting my relationships.

Many children, in the U.S., are raised in single-parent households. It has been a common occurrence for many families, and even worse for generations that understand the impact of the baby daddy. In my attempts to analyze the instances of how baby daddies have impacted my life, I am hoping to educate the many men and women, who look for spouses as they climb the corporate and social ladders. It is evident for many minority executives that as they climb the corporate ladders and excel in educational opportunities that the availability of minority men or women decreases.

It has been my experience that as I completed many levels of my education, the female counterparts that I would meet were going in different directions. As I struggled to find single, professional, physician women to date, it was amazing to find that the pool of available physicians and professionals were surprisingly small. The higher I went, the less opportunity there was to date. Nonetheless, I did find that there was one segment of the population that was always busy and had various opportunities for dating. This segment often caused great lifestyle changes and devastating effects to entire communities. This micro-population of the baby daddy had a special talent of seducing women to fall in love with them and have unprotected sex. Most times, leaving their prey with children to raise by themselves, usually in an economically-depressed state.

Many of these men are products of single-parent homes themselves and develop selfish mindsets that prevent their involvement in a committed relationship. Many of these men had no father in the home to act as a good, male role model. Usually, baby daddies have made their presence known in our community. They can be seen in our churches, schools and, obviously, in the single-parent households that are headed predominantly by females. My story envelops the phenomenon of the baby daddy and how he/it affected my life. More importantly, it demonstrates my triumph of overcoming the barriers that lead many men and women into the generational stigma and/or trap of dealing with a baby daddy invasion.

2
How I met my wife

This is a really unique way to discuss how I met my wife Rachel. I had just finished with my board exams, and I was on my "southern tour," as I had called it. I was visiting family in Seneca, S.C., while also visiting my alma mater, Morris College, in Sumter, where I received my BS degree in Biology. I have quite a few friends in the area, as well as many church families, whom I enjoy visiting from time to time.

I had a great homecoming as I was visiting friends. It is always a great thing to have friends and a home base to touch when you lived a great portion of your adult life looking for stability. I was looking forward to turning over a new leaf, and I was tired of being scared of approaching women and getting the "short end" of the stick. I had tried approaching a few women at clubs and even in appropriate social venues like galas and network outings. It seemed that sometimes women would look at me like I was not attractive enough. Some females even made me feel like I was a fool or as many of my colleagues would put it, "You just got your game shot down."

It was then that I decided to shake off the shame of having my pride hurt. I also found that I was trying to get over the past hurt that consistently haunted me, even when I took a glance at a pretty woman. I was attempting to recover my manhood and rekindle my dating life. I figured that at this point, there was nothing left to lose. I had also matured from the young man that I used to be. After passing my boards, I was in the mood to just have fun and let my hair down. So, going back to visit family and friends in South Carolina always seemed like a great idea, when getting back to myself was the agenda. Being down south is very therapeutic. You can experience real southern food, genuine kindness, great family traditions and wonderful people.

I was really in search of the "treasured assets" of southern culture, as I drove across the rural highways of South Carolina, in search of my life-changing experience. I went to a local church that I frequently visited called *Church of God by Faith*. I went there primarily to say hello to the congregation and fellowship. It was

November 29, 2002. On this particular Sunday morning, a very nice woman, whom I had met while attending Morris College, was accompanied by a beautiful, young woman. Although I was in church for worship, I couldn't take my eyes off of this girl.   I kept rationalizing that this lovely, young lady was obviously the daughter, friend or some relative.

I must admit that when the pastor asked me to have words at the morning service, I did not expect to be smitten by this lovely, young lady. I was surprised to see a young, attractive woman at the church, on the Sunday just following the Thanksgiving holiday. Church of God by Faith was a rural, southern traditional church, with an older African-American congregation. I simply enjoyed the people and the 'real love' I felt when I would frequently attend this little church that boasted an authentic worship and southern- style, African-American gospel choir.

The pastor asked me to come up and share some words with the congregation, I did. This was a time for me to reflect and talk about how the Lord had delivered me through my board exam. I felt free and safe from ridicule, whenever I expressed myself in God at the church. It was safe haven, where I knew I would never be judged or made fun of. It was a good place to be honest, give encouragement and gain strength for my soul, all at the same time.

As I spoke to the church, I couldn't help but to notice the glances of this young lady, whose eyes appeared to be glued on me. Frankly, she was very attractive. She had on a lovely blue dress and her hair was hanging down her back. It was black, thick and lovely in appearance. Her skin was clear and without blemish. She had a lovely, light golden-brown complexion, with big, brown eyes. Her eyes were on my every move, and I could tell that she was in sync with me as I began to speak to the congregation.

After the pastor spoke, I went over to speak to the woman I had previously known.

After our brief conversation, she said, "I'd like to introduce you to my daughter, Rachel."

Her mother explained that Rachel had gone to Francis Marion University, a local University located in Florence, South Carolina. Rachel's mother began to tell me that Rachel was living in Charlotte,

N.C. and that she was a good person. It seemed like her mother was ushering our conversation, so that Rachel and I did not have to say much, but our eyes said it all. There was a small silence and inter-locking space of attraction between us. This was the kind of attraction you only get when you are in the moment of the unknown and every moment, thereafter, is out of your control.

Rachel and I exchanged phone numbers, and we politely allowed worship service to resume. It was at this moment that I remembered that I was only supposed to be at Church of God by Faith for a brief moment. This was because I was supposed to be traveling to another church service that was going on down the road. This other church also had great friends and colleagues, in whom I missed and wanted to catch up with. In the south, church is a unique institution where you can see and chat with all of your local friends because most people of faith, in the south, go to church. Church is like a weekly meeting place for businesses, fraternities, sororities and community activities. In the African-American experience, church was the absolute gathering where all dignitaries, even the non-spiritual, became equals, as we were all in need of mercy from God. Consequently, we all have done some form of sin, one way or another. None of us are above reproach in our faith, according to how I was raised to believe in God.

I proceeded to leave the church where I met Rachel, in order to go to another church in Sumter, S.C. I began to think to myself that I never seemed to follow up on anything when it came to a beautiful woman. My mind went to an encounter that I had with a beautiful lady in Cleveland, Ohio one day after a Sunday service. I was in the lobby area at this particular church: *Mount Olive Institutional Baptist church.* The pastor was an eloquent speaker by the name of Dr. Otis Moss, Sr. After a great sermon, there was always a gathering, where the congregation would fellowship. This would take place in an area where paintings and art work were displayed on the civil rights era. Great historical portraits and artifacts were laid out for people to purchase or observe and fellowship around. My eye caught a beam from a beautiful, young woman. She had very fair skin and long, beautiful black hair. She stood about 5'6" and was well built. She was not fat or disproportioned, but womanly endowed in her red classy dress.

I must admit that I was taken. As I could sometimes be "star struck" in the presence of such a beautiful lady, she actually moved close to me, almost within arm's reach, as if to position herself to speak to me. I just simply (and stupidly) acted as if I was reading a brochure when in reality; I was unsure of myself and scared to death to say anything. According to my social history, I was always "shot down" or embarrassed, and I did not want to make a move and risk getting embarrassed again. God in heaven knows I only wished that my courage was within me at that moment. Unfortunately, my courage failed and as I looked up again, she was gone. I went to the exit of the church and saw her walking with a female companion (probably her mother). I wanted to introduce myself, but it was then that I knew that I had lost a chance of a lifetime. I felt the drive and a strong tug in my chest to speak, but the moment had escaped. I returned to the church, Sunday after Sunday, hoping to see her again. I felt that I had possibly missed out on a great opportunity, yet I was determined to see her again—to have that moment back. After going back to that church, for almost two months, I never saw her again.

I often wondered who she was and why I felt drawn to her. Why did I feel such a passion to speak, when I did not know her? After the disappearance of this "mystery woman," I vowed, despite the fear of rejection, that I would never let another woman get away from me. I promised that I would, at least, take the chance to introduce myself.

I often wondered if she could have been my wife or some special women that I was supposed to know. Unfortunately, I never got the answer to this question. The question still weighed heavily on my mind, even as I drove from the church, after meeting Rachel. I turned the corner heading back to Sumter when, suddenly, something made me turn around. I needed to find out who Rachel was and where the road might lead.

I remember asking myself, "What do I have to loose?"

It was then that I grew some short, but sustainable "balls of manhood." This would allow me to withstand Rachel's rejection, if it came to that. Nevertheless, I was determined to investigate and see what life possibly had in store. I could not make the same mistake as before and live without ever knowing the outcome. So I turned my car around, right in the middle of the road, and decided to follow up on my attraction to Rachel. After the church service, I approached Rachel and her mother and began to reintroduce myself. I asked Rachel where she lived and what she did for a living. This line of questioning ultimately led to me asking her if she was free for dinner. She was sitting in her car and her Mother mentioned that they were headed to her Grandmother's place for dinner. They asked for me to join them and I accepted. After all, it was the weekend after Thanksgiving, so food was still abundant. I remember thinking that I could use some good, southern home cooked food.

Amazingly, I felt relieved of my fears, especially since I did not get shot down or made the butt-end of a joke. I felt that I had hit the jack pot—I was like yes! A real date, on the first real step of faith. I took a chance to show some real interest in a female and she responded with kindness and gracefulness. I was not too fat or too tall or too Black for that matter. While following her car, I felt that this was the best moment ever. It felt good because I was finally overcoming my self-contained fear of the unknown. This life experience allowed me to enjoy the door that courage opened. Overcoming the fear of rejection had suddenly released me to approach Rachel. Rachel did not tell me that she was seeing anyone, and I did not see a ring on her finger. Any good man will always check for these things when approaching a female. She never conversed about any commitment, and I felt good talking to her. So the situation presented itself perfect, and I was just thankful to God for allowing me to have a moment of courage for once in my life. This would allow me to become fruitful and never again feel the stinging darts of embarrassment. This boost to my ego would never allow me to feel terrible about myself again.

As we finally reached her Grandmother's house, I found it to be small, but big with family and friends. This scene was familiar to me, as I often visited the church many times and frequently spent time with church members who were related to Rachel. The food was superb, as usual, and I offered to take Rachel to the movies. We had a nice time. I actually paid, as all gentlemen should on the first date, especially if you initiate the idea of going out. After the show, we got back in Rachel's car and drove to her house. At the time, she lived with her mother. I left my car to save on gas and to get a little closer to Rachel. As I wanted to dialogue and get to know her, I recall how I could not stop admiring her beauty and how lucky I felt. I felt that she could be "the one" and maybe God had finally given me a break. I could possibly begin to establish some great communication with a beautiful girl who was nice, single and by all sense of the word attractive. She was available. With no other man in sight or any attachment, this evening of great courage for me began to conclude. As Rachel was driving down the road, we began to talk about life and our plans. I was single and she was too.

Out of nowhere, Rachel said to me, "Mark, I want you to know something about me...I am expecting."

I replied, "Expecting what?"

Rachel continued by saying, "I am expecting to have a baby soon—I am with child."

I cannot tell you how I felt at this very moment. I exclaimed, "What! You didn't tell me this earlier today."

Rachel replied, "I didn't know how to tell you, and I wanted you to know. I'm sorry if you feel bad. Please don't be disappointed with me."

At this point I was numb. Soon, those old feelings of embarrassment, coupled with the feelings of someone trying to get over on me, suddenly began rushing back. I felt like a fool, and I felt as if I was in a situation that I could have avoided altogether—if I had only kept driving to Sumter.

My worst fears were coming true. It seemed that whenever I would approach a woman and seemingly give my all—not play any games and just come with the real me—something cruel seemed to always happen. This was proof all over again. I tried to play off my embarrassment and frustration as best I could. When I thought that Rachel was, perhaps, 'playing me off,' that frustrated me even further. I was hurt from putting myself out there like this.

I felt like a fool, while all the time wondering, "Wow! How could this happen to me today?"

We finally arrived at her mom's house, with the mood being shattered moments before. We sat silently in her car for about a minute or so. I could not hear myself think, yet, somehow, I thought about what I could say to get past this moment and get the hell out of this situation? What was worse was that I knew her family, so I had to, at least, keep a good relationship with them. This prevented me from straight cussin' Rachel out, which I could have done, if I had not known her family. So out of the blue, she invited me into the house and offered me a plate of food to go for my journey back to Sumter. Suddenly, there was a phone call from her baby's daddy. I was further embarrassed because she had told me that she was not involved with anyone earlier that day.

Their phone call lasted briefly, as she posed to her baby's daddy, "What do you want? Why are you calling me if you don't want or have anything? I'm hanging up now if you're not calling for anything."

Rachel turned to me and asked, "Are you going to let a phone call scare you away?" Rachel continued. "My relationship with my baby daddy is over, and we are not involved anymore. I'm having his child, but we are not together. I know you didn't expect this to happen, but this situation is for real."

Actually, I remember thinking to myself, "What the hell did I get myself into now?"

My thought was how could a beautiful girl get involved with a low-life like this? This guy didn't present himself worthy of a good person like Rachel. Rachel and I went into her mom's house, and she began to fix my plate of barbequed pork chops, collard greens and rice.

If you are from the south, then you know how women cook down here. I could not wrap my consciousness around Rachel being pregnant, and I felt both confused and used. I actually reached out and touched Rachel's lower abdominal area gently, very gently. Rachel allowed me to touch her, but in a very cautious way. She knew that I was feeling for proof of her pregnancy, and she wanted me to know that she was being honest. With the gentle touch of her warm, soft lower stomach, I knew that she had life inside of her. I knew from that moment that I would never be the same.

I met a beautiful girl on whom I took a chance. Introducing myself to her turned out to be a *Nightmare on Elm Street* kind-of-event. I was excited but humiliated. I felt played and belittled because she could have told me her situation from jump street. She had the opportunity to tell me at the church, or even at her grandmother's house. But to let me take her to the movies, knowing all along that she was with child? "Expecting," as she put it, made me feel like Rachel took me for a ride. The fact that she was pregnant made me feel that she just wanted to get out of the house. She wanted to have her cake and eat it too.

I then thought about how she had become a victim of her baby daddy's deception and games that no-good, African-American men have been playing for centuries on women. I began to think that Rachel had just been 'caught up' in her own lust and perceptions of a man, whom she once thought to be a nice guy, but had really fallen in love with a thug. All these thoughts raced through my mind, and I went from feeling sad for Rachel to feeling angry and played. As a man who was truthful, when approaching women, she had just taken advantage of my goodness and played on my attraction for her. "That Bitch!" I said to myself.

Finally, I got my plate of food and was heading out. Rachel and I sat back in her car since she had to back up, in order to let me out of the driveway. We chatted for a second about nothing. Our casual exchange allowed us to pass the moment, as she backed her car out of the driveway.

I said to Rachel, "I have never been in a situation like this before. You are pregnant and very attractive. I don't know what to do with this tonight?"

Rachel replied, "I know you were not looking for this from me, but I was not looking for this for myself. I feel bad sometimes— the way this happened—because this was not planned at all."

For a moment it was dead silence between us. We both realized that life would never be the same for either of us. It was as if time had caught both of us, allowed us to meet and shown us how alone we both were. We could feel one another's disappointment with life and had many questions of the what, when and how. Consequently, we had few answers in our moments of silence, in the car. I leaned over and kissed Rachel on her cheek, and we hugged each other with a warm embrace. I got in my car and she led me out to highway 76 back to Sumter. I watched her in my rear view mirror, as she turned around to head back to her mom's place.

At that moment, I remember thinking to myself, "…Wow, what the hell happened to me today?"

I was thoroughly amazed from our conversation, her embrace of me and the fact that we could talk to one another, even in this unexpected situation. My curiosity and frustration grew strong. I wanted revenge for being played. I felt foolish and basically cursed myself for turning my car around, earlier that day. It was a short ride back to Sumter, but in my mind, this experience made the trip seem like a million miles. As I pondered the next phase of my life, all I could think of was how beautiful Rachel was and how I felt whenever I talked to her. She understood me. And although she initially appeared honest, this new turn of events ushered in a shadow that made her seem somewhat deceiving and distant. But what can you expect from meeting a woman that had her life invaded by a baby daddy? She had been victimized by her own lust and deceived by a man who claimed that he loved her and promised her the world.

It seemed that Rachel and I had more in common than we could ever imagine. We had both been played by life and bad people. I could only wish that things would have been different between us from that night. Nonetheless, I knew that something special had happened when I met her. I left her feeling frustrated, excited, confused, humiliated, but most of all—mad as hell! I have felt many things but never an emotional rush like this. With all my senses heightened, my mind was racing a mile-a-minute over this woman and her situation. It was both strange and bizarre to encounter, yet I could hardly sleep that night. All I could do was think about my day with Rachel and how crazy she made me feel. I was wondering about her as I returned to Cleveland, Ohio, and, ironically, I found her phone number. About two weeks later, I finally built up the nerve to call, once my anger and frustration had subsided. I knew that I was facing a challenge, but only God knew where it would lead me. Life had drastically changed for me, and I knew that things would never be the same from that night on. Life is crazy when you open up to the wild, frustrating, confusing excitement that can also prove to be humiliating. Just so happens, it was like that on the day I met Rachel.

3
What expecting means to a relationship

It is a true concept that men may never admit, but know that most men like a challenge of something new. My challenge was entertaining a woman that was with child, and that hit me like a ton of bricks. My reaction was unexpected. Most guys would have probably run for the hills and "got the hell out of dodge," as the old saying goes. Nonetheless, I am the kind of person who, for some odd reason, seems to always, courageously climb the mountains of life, while continually getting the 'short-end' of the stick. Well, believe it or not, when I called Rachel, I knew that she was with child—sometimes I honestly don't know why I called back. Maybe it was just to be her friend, or maybe I was so attracted to her that her being pregnant did not matter to me. I had no clue of what a pregnant woman was all about, and I guess I was more curious about her life than anything. I honestly have to admit, for my own integrity, that I was sexually attracted to Rachel, as she did not even look pregnant. She looked incredible, and part of me just wanted to have some crazy sex with her. As I could not even fathom her pregnancy, I had to face the reality that she was not some average lady from the street who I could just "hook up" with, have a sexual encounter and be out the door. It seemed as we began to talk more frequently, my affinity for Rachel began to grow. She slowly became a friend and, more importantly, someone, while even though pregnant, of great interest to me.

I began to slowly let go of my sexual attraction, (i.e., mentality) and began to see the whole woman, and the emotional bond being created between us. All the while, I had to keep in mind that I could not have sex with her for two reasons. First, Rachel was in Charlotte. Second, she was carrying a child, who did not belong to me. Rachel and I were not on that level. I was normally sexually attracted to women to whom I could not express myself. Most men could only begin to imagine how frustrating it can be to endeavor a long-distance, phone relationship that existed for about six months. After the first month of communicating, I felt the intertwining of our fate. She and I began to chat about her life and what she endured, while being pregnant. She would continuously tell me how much I meant to her and how she would anticipate my phone calls. We would often discuss her relationship with her baby's daddy and how the relationship barely existed. As our relationship grew, Rachel explained how she barely spoke to her baby's daddy, except through random phone calls that she often missed.

I began to think that this guy would eventually drop his connection to this beautiful woman. I could tell that Rachel was hurt every time that we spoke about her previous relationship. It took her to a place, where only a woman, who has been hurt, could understand. I tried to understand the situation, but I suppose that being a single guy with no children, nor a record of being a baby daddy, it was evident that I was just on the outside looking in.

I realized that my attraction for Rachel was increasing. I strongly believe that this was attributed to both the emotional and psychological relief that I was able to provide to Rachel, during her pregnancy. Consequently, Rachel still had emotional ties to her baby's daddy. This reality was very painful for her. I saw her as a victim with an unrealistic view of her baby's daddy. Furthermore, it became evident that she was irresponsible in protecting herself from both the pregnancy, and the emotional instability of a man whom she knew did not care for her. Her mentality was that she could 'change him' by being a good woman. Consequently, like many women with this mentality, she got played. This further added insult to injury to the deceit and lies that she heard many times. This clarified my position; as I continued to serve as a great relief counselor, friend and confidant. I provided a successful alternative to living with a selfish man who walked out on his child. It behooved me that in his doing so, he was able to maintain a strong, mental control on the baby's mama. I can not say why I was so intrigued by all this drama, but I suppose in thinking about it, I began to feel as if life had taken a crap on me. My own life was not so different. Although I did not have any children, I did have the emotional scars and memories to deal with that were usually just as forceful—like a blow to the body.

Rachel and I had a lot in common from life's let downs. This was our bond that transformed me from lusting; to understanding her, and the good that she represented.

I can still hear her telling me that "She never thought she would be in this situation," and how "She often felt boxed in with her decision to keep the baby."

We discussed her decision and how she felt that having a baby would "seal the deal" with her baby daddy. It also seemed that Rachel had some challenges with abortion and did not want to travel down that road.

As a man, I can see how emotionally perplexing this situation could be for a woman. I thought of my own mother, who was also a single parent and how she did not abort me or my other siblings. She loved me before I was born and, ultimately, lived in the hope that I could make something out of myself. In the end, she maintained her faith that God would bless me. My mother often called me her 'blessed child' because I was prayed for and blessed in the womb. It was these memories that ran through my mind when speaking quite regularly to Rachel and hearing her daily living log of what she desired. Maybe I felt sorry for Rachel, yet, more importantly, I was her hero. I was a healthy alternative who proved to be special. Moreover, I was a person of importance to Rachel. It felt good to be needed by her, as this was a first for me. Although she was with child, I knew that I was more of a man to Rachel than I was to any other woman that I had ever met. She gave me what I was looking for, and that was all the reason that I needed to get involved. Looking back, I only hope that my life actually had purpose and meaning

By now, it was spring and Rachel was in her ninth month. I was in Cleveland finishing up my studies at medical school, at the Ohio College of Podiatric Medicine. As I prepared for graduation, I did not tell anybody about Rachel. I was not ashamed of her, but I knew that it would be hard to discuss without having been administered the "third degree." Our relationship was strictly over the phone, and we had no physical contact, from the day we met. We shared a mental connection and developed a great phone relationship, which I had come to appreciate. As I was still dating and having casual, protected sex here and there, nothing serious enough ever came about to replace my evening phone chats with Rachel. No female came along with a mental connection to match Rachel.

Ironically, Rachel and I were not dating each other. I often wished that some of the women were mentally like Rachel, but I was never successful in coming close to friendship that we had developed.

I often wished that I would have met a beautiful woman with no children. Maybe I was selfish, but I wanted to be the first man to give a woman life. I wanted to be faithful and have a wonderful life with someone in whom I could develop purpose. God knows that as a single man, I always looked for this, and I guess in looking, I seemed to miss the "good" single women. It seems that when you are single, everybody always seems to be committed. As the old saying goes, "all the good ones are taken." As a result of my observations, I made up another saying, "All the good women are pregnant or have babies with baby daddies." Now neither of these sayings are valid, but they are sayings out of frustration, deceit, pain and disappointment.

It has always been said that many men are dogs. My disbelief in this statement is not only because I am a man, but because I am not a dog, nor do I perform dog-like behavior toward women. Nonetheless, I do not think that most women are whores. Occasionally, it just seems that many of the women that I have met have had unprotected sex in multiple relationships. But this also applies to men as well because for every woman that has a child or children it took a man to give them to her. If women are going to be stained then society has to spread the blame to impact the men as well. In my findings, it seems that society's detrimental view toward women has always been one-sided. This holds especially true in instances where women are left 'holding the bag,' after one night of intimate pleasure. As I am also guilty of carnal pleasure, it would be inauthentic to write such a powerful statement without the mention of my own lust and the power of the illusion of sexual gratification. I truly believe that most single guys really want a thrill—a real passion with most of the women they encounter sexually. I would like to know how a woman feels sexually, especially if I dance with her. It is sexually stimulating to watch a well-built woman, not fat or skinny, dance. Generally, she possesses a great sexual allure. Men, throughout the ages, would agree that a woman with full lips, great hips and lovely mocha, smooth skin is tantalizing to say the least. This is especially true, if she is dancing, with natural, beautiful hair. I was looking for a lovely single lady with no children, educated, God-loving and family oriented. I was also excited that I could go anywhere to start a new life. This sounded fantastic, but reality has a way of always stepping into our existence and showing us a different path.

As man wrestles with his manhood and sexual attraction to women, it becomes a real assignment to find a relationship that works. It often confused me when people would ask me to find someone without children, or a woman who was ready to settle down. I think the familiar statement that would always blow me away was, "…you will know when you have found the right one for you, it will be just right and it will certainly come to you."

I was always thinking that a light from heaven would shine down on the woman from within the crowd and I would hear this confirming voice from heaven. It would be then that I would know that I stood on hollow ground. This was not my situation, and I do not think that most people really think this happens in real life—only in the movies or in the videos. In most instances, in meeting someone nice, two thoughts would usually come to mind. First, I would think to myself that she is a nice girl, and I would like to get to know her. In contrast, the other thought would often include my wanting to have some passionate sex with this attractive, warm girl that gave me some conversation. I would often imagine that the woman would be sweet to experience sexually.

I was involved in a whirlwind of emotions and seemed to feel every part of my heart as I continued to talk to Rachel. She did not know that I wanted her in this fashion or with so much passion, but I yearned for her during our hours of conversation, which occurred two to three times per week. Honestly, my casual sexual encounters felt good. Don't get me wrong! After all, it was sex with a woman. But I was so mentally in tune with Rachel that I would fantasize about being with Rachel, while being intimate with other women. It began to dawn on me that I was really being drawn into Rachel a great deal, and I was not sure where she and I were going in our escapades of phone calls and mental togetherness. I surprised myself that I even kept talking to Rachel. Although she was not what I initially wanted, while completing medical school, I couldn't keep her off of my mind.

While starting my residency training in Pennsylvania, Rachel delivered her son. We had spent time choosing baby names about two weeks before she delivered. I joked with her that she would name the baby after the baby daddy because I felt that she still had feelings for him.

She adamantly said, "No I am not going to name the child after that nigga! I'll use another name!"

Well, just as I thought, she stuck with the ignorant southern tradition of naming her son after the baby's daddy, even after he denied his own child.

This tradition of naming the child after the baby's daddy is a common one and most times the woman never marries the child's father. This is why I call this tradition ignorant. Unfortunately, it is a tradition that is killing the integrity of the family, in the African-American community. Especially as it relates to the woman, who grows up from this point and realizes that she is ready to actually meet a real man and get married. They are forever reminded of how crazy their idea was to name their child after someone who not only excludes himself from the life of the child, but really never plans to contribute to the life of the child, in the first place. Moreover, the relationship with the baby's mother is usually abandoned and left destitute.

Rachel has always regretted her decision to name her son after the baby's daddy. It's something that often produces tears when she thinks about what she did. I believe she thought that somehow there was a chance of happiness with her baby's daddy. I felt her pain and emotional scars. As she would call the child by his middle name, this allowed her temporary escape from the mistake of naming her child after her baby's daddy. This is typical of many women who have named their children after their baby's father. Usually, in these cases, the child will have a nickname or even use a middle name. I have had family members who have also been victims of this common tradition that pays no dividends. It is sometimes disheartening to realize that these instances often end up as the butt-end of jokes about African-American culture. At times I believe if we did not have some positive outlet from our pain, then we would cry uncontrollably.

At this point, a man has to make a decision of what he will

deal with in life. I was coming toward that decision, and I had to look at considering where Rachel and I would eventually go from here. I was in Pennsylvania now and starting my residency training. Rachel had moved to her own apartment and was recovering well from her delivery. Rachel and I planned to see each other as I drove down to South Carolina to visit relatives. I visited her at her mom's place in Florence, S.C. It had been 4 months since her delivery and she was looking good.

Rachel and I embraced each other, and it felt as if I was seeing someone I had known my entire life. I could tell that Rachel's physical appearance had slightly changed. I noticed that she had gained just a little bit in her breast area and mildly everywhere else. The sister was thick where it counted. Rachel looked great as she wore a burgundy button top with khaki pants that fit her well. Her hair was in curls and hanging in thick locks, and her skin was as beautiful as it was on the first day we met. Her beautiful big brown eyes were glad to see me, and I could tell that she was happy with the smile that she had on her face. Rachel met me at a local hotel, as we just admired each other for a good amount of time. My words were temporarily taken from me, as she stood in front of me. She was my vision of fantasy, and I was rushed with emotion.

We sat and talked in my hotel room about what I had been doing.

Rachel asked, "Have you had a long trip today? I waited for you all day, and I'm sorry that I did not cook anything, but I will have dinner for you tomorrow."

I replied, "It's good to see that southern hospitality is still yet alive. You look great. I'm sorry I got here late this evening. I got lost in the West Virginia mountains, but you were worth the drive."

I could see from Rachel's smile that my words were soothing to her expectations of my arrival. It was great to see her smile and to be back in her presence, after about 6 months of having a phone relationship. As we sat in my room, I wanted her right away. I was overjoyed to see her.

Rachel asked, "Do I look the same as you remembered me? I have changed a little from the pregnancy, but I am trying to get back in shape—just letting my body recover."

I replied, "Rachel, you are beautiful you know a little weight gain is expected after a pregnancy. I'm taken to just be in your presence...it's good to see you after all this time."

Rachel and I embraced and kissed. That kiss was sweet to me, as I felt it throughout my soul. I wanted more, but Rachel was on her guard, as she began to slow me down. I did not mind because I respected her more for that gesture. Rachel told me that she would be content with just sitting with me and catching up on old times. We chatted for a while, and I could tell that she was hanging on my every word. We talked about my travels and the challenges of my medical career.

I sat across from her, as I talked about the last six months of completing medical school and my residency in Pennsylvania. It was great to look at her and exchange laughs. It felt the same, as if we were back on the phone, except we were now face-to-face. Truthfully, I believe that Rachel was just as aroused as I was. Nonetheless, we continued to converse. As the night ended, we embraced once again and kissed passionately. It was truthfully heartfelt and was as wonderful as our first kiss all over again. I felt great, and I was overly excited for the next day to arrive, so I could spend more time with Rachel and get some good home cooked food. Nothing is better than a home cooked meal, and I consider myself to be at home whenever I am in the south. Rachel got into her car and headed back to her mom's place. Meanwhile, I relaxed in the hotel bed and looked forward to the next day.

Rachel called me early the next morning and said, "Hello, Mark, are you hungry? I'm cooking breakfast this morning for you. We have grits, bacon, eggs, toast and some juice. I know you're ready for some good southern food, so mom and I are preparing you a good meal to start our day."

I replied, "Oh yeah! I've been waiting on this southern hospitality to roll my way. I'm very hungry and ready to eat. I can be ready in about half an hour."

Rachel replied, "I'm so happy to have you here, and I know you like southern food. You're gonna love this food today. I'll be there to pick you up soon."

It felt so good to get that phone call and just to know that someone was thinking about me in that way was even more special. I got up and immediately began to shower and look forward to the good meal that was to come. I was on vacation and all seemed well. I felt that life was great knowing that I would be with Rachel soon. It is a great emotional boost when you feel things working out in your favor. Perhaps the stars and the wind are working well for once and nothing can go wrong. I felt like everything was actually right with the universe. It was good to know that a brother had a southern meal coming to him.

I remember thinking, "It just doesn't get any better than this." I was hungry and ready for the free, homemade meal.

When Rachel took me to her mother's house, we ate breakfast and sat around enjoying each other's company. We talked more intimately on all topics that included her little son that had awakened and filled the house with his cries. For the first time, I observed Rachel's performance as a mother, and it proved to be quite a humbling experience. Rachel's son was a few months old. His little cries for life attention, along with the occasional diaper change was very entertaining. I had never been around her and her son, so I really felt like I was imposing on her mommy time. It was different seeing her in this light. I did not feel threatened by her child. After all, I knew that Rachel had been pregnant when I first met her, but the impression of seeing her child, who belonged to another man, really hit home. I began to feel out of place, as I looked at the little baby. Furthermore, it seemed that I would never get to know Rachel in the way that her baby's daddy did.

It had been 6 months since I last saw Rachel. The last time that we were together, she did not have a baby nor did she look pregnant. So part of my mind was still holding on to the lady that I knew 6 months ago. Consequently, I still enjoyed being in Rachel's presence. I wanted her intimately, even more as I watched her being a mother. I found it attractive, even though I knew a baby daddy had been there before me. I was simply into the woman Rachel represented. The reality was that Rachel and I had developed a 6-month communication channel that had really grown into something. I was actually content with our continued relationship. Seeing her let me know that she was also over her baby's daddy and was open to me, as I was to her. I knew that we would have a good time, as we ate the good breakfast that Rachel and her mother cooked.

Rachel's mother was glad to see me as we sat at the kitchen table and talked about my travels. I felt good, and Rachel put her son in my arms. As I held the little baby, he began to go to sleep. After breakfast, the baby was well asleep, and Rachel and I shared some private time. As we sat down, I could feel her carnal desire for me. I observed her look of happiness and satisfaction. As she felt comfortable having her son around me, she became confident that I was not there to play with her emotions, nor was only interested in sex.

I was pleased to see that our 6 months of talking to each other added credibility to this day. We were comfortable with each other. Rachel's mother left to go to work, leaving us alone with a sleeping baby. The house was silent, as if all sound had left with her mother. I knew that Rachel did not want to seem easy to have sex, or to have me thrown upon her like some wild animal, so I just watched T.V. for a moment, but all the while I was checking her out.

Rachel said, "Are you glad that you came down here to see me today? Was the food good?"

I replied, "Oh, yeah! I'm very happy that I came down today. It's a trip to finally see your little man that's been in the making for sometime now. By the way, the food was great—nothing like home cooking."

Rachel looked in my eyes and asked, "Do you still see me like the person you talked to over the phone, even though I have a child now?"

I could tell that Rachel was thinking this all along, and it was just like her to be straight forward when she wanted to get to the bottom of something.

I replied, "Rachel, I knew you were pregnant after you told me the first day I met you. I've known all along that you would be a mother. I was afraid at first, but Rachel, with you I feel good. I'm happy to be here. There's no other place that I'd rather be right now."

All I could hear was the air conditioner blowing in the background as Rachel looked at me and moved in my direction to set the moment for an embrace. I was certainly taken by the rush of emotions that I felt, and I knew that this was the right moment. I held Rachel as she fell into my arms. Her body was warm and firm, yet soft and gentle. We kissed passionately, as I felt my manhood rise to the occasion. I had a feeling that this could turn into something but only time would tell.

4
Everyone, yet no one really knows

I am always amazed at how my friends knew about everything that I was going through with seeing Rachel. I had heard of everything from, "Man, you must be crazy!" to "Mark, you should really leave it alone," or "That will be a nightmare, and it will never work." I was confused, and I am sure that with all that I had been through, this was probably my greatest test of maturity in matters of the heart. Don't get me wrong. I treasure my friends and family's advice, and I never take it lightly. But when it came to Rachel, no one else's opinion really mattered.

Many of my friends would point out to me that I was not getting any younger and that my biological clock was ticking. Yes, men have these too. I often reflected on those conversations by saying to myself, "Wow, one can be very confused with hearing so much chatter about how everyone knows what is right for you." I am always open to criticism from those who have been in my shoes, but as usual, there are very few people who've ever been there (or at least, I think so). The great debate about life is you have to have experience to tell it. If you've never been there, you can't talk. It was often hard to hear so many people speak about what they would do in my situation. Usually, they were already married to a great wife who had no children. Sometimes their marriages seemed as if they had been great forever. In the end, my relationship with both Rachel and her child seemed like an abomination and out of sync with the normal rhythm of life. Naturally, this was how I felt, at first, as I compared my situation to others.

It was great to hear the many different stories that people contributed, from time to time. Let me also take time here to thank all those who gave me advice and counsel at the critical times where I needed a good word of encouragement. For those individuals and family, I will forever be grateful.

I must point out that many people are always interested in the human struggle and the life challenges of other people. It seems that the phenomenon of the curiosity of the human condition is continuous. Its dynamics touch everything from lust, deceit, love and

38

anger. These emotions especially existed in relationships where a woman, who already had a child (with a babby's daddy), was evident. My observations pointed to the high frequency of single-parent households in the African-American community. Prior to this painstaking epiphany, I never knew why many attractive women, with kids in my church or community, never got married? I used to think it was church rule or something, where men and women felt as if no one wanted to marry them. This belief haunted my thoughts for many nights, as I pondered my growing affection for both Rachel and her son. I always wondered why my mother never got married. Especially, since she had custody of her children. This dysfunctional phenomenon is abundant throughout the African-American community. It is coupled with the statistic that the United States has, at least, a 70% population of unwed or single-parent, African American families. Reasons for African American inclusion to this denigrating statistic can be attributed to: low socio-economics, poor parenting skills, irresponsibility and/or denial of a child's existence. Over time, many people develop coping mechanisms, which allow them to endure this abnormality.

Although I was raised in a single-family household, I always wanted to have a good relationship with my father. Unfortunately, that never happened. I would never experience the natural joy of a father figure because my father died shortly after my birth. To date, I have never seen a photo of my father. What was worse was that my mother didn't even know him very well. This is evident of how young, African-American people can "get around" in their community. This also showed me how there is a lack of courtship and "getting to know you," before sexual encounters take place. Consequently, it is very difficult to walk out on someone that you love and trust versus someone that you meet for a one-night stand. It behooves how women seem to be the most responsible when indiscretions produce illegitimate children. Statistically speaking, they (women) get custody, while the man (i.e., baby daddy) is free to abandon the family.

My observations have always shown that women are the glue that holds the family together. Perhaps this mentality can be referenced to slavery, as it was then that families were separated to provide more slaves to other plantations. White slave masters never took in to account the legitimacy of the African American family. Many researchers and historians of African-American culture agree that slavery displaced the African-American male from his natural role as 'head of household.' As the institution of slavery has been abolished now for over 200 hundred years, my question still stands, "Why do most African-American men abandon their families/children and never marry to keep the family together?" To contest my own question, if slavery can be attributed as an excuse for the baby daddy syndrome, for the African-American male, then how do we explain today's abandonment issues, as there are no more slave masters to blame?

I am uncertain if there is an answer for this question; nonetheless, the contemporary baby daddy syndrome demonstrates the accepted values that transcend from one generation to the next. Furthermore, it emphasizes that our women and men are not yet getting to the heart of sustaining a successful relationship. This cancer slowly kills the sanctity of marriage, especially in the African-American family.

Many think this is hearsay, but until you live life looking for love, a spouse and family; this reality is a daily fight. Previous African American generations have passed down a curse of selfishness and cultural suicide that seemingly accepts irresponsibility and wayward invasions of family (i.e., like the baby daddy). The white slave master has been abolished by law; however, the contemporary slave master is now the African-American male, himself. These cultural cowards who defame the family-oriented African American man, paint society's accepted norm of the black man who abandons his home, without chains or whips. Ultimately, full acceptance of this stereotype robs the male of his rightful place in the lives of the next generation.

It is unique to the African-American community that men have had the right to parent at will, and women parent out of responsibility. It is the only answer to how the black family structure has endured for over the last half century in America. Most historians agree that it is extremely difficult to trace the lineage of African-Americans because of the institution of slavery. Today, this disconnect can be attributed to the irresponsibility of sexual relationships and abandonment of children, usually perpetrated by the African American baby daddy.

Many people want to believe that a mother and father will get along for the sake of the child. Consequently, the many relationship challenges, personal insecurities and maturity factors prevent this from happening. Furthermore, it is evident that the African-American community produces an abundance of these "love-hate" relationships, even when the mother has moved on and realizes that the baby daddy engages in invasive, 'at will' tactics. As a result of these actions, the mother, in order to establish some form of paternal consistency, will support a court-mandated paternity test to legally establish paternity and child support.

Most men, who are not in a marital relationship, before becoming a father, will often find it easy to abandon both the child and mother. This is because the father envisions the mother as both the root of his problem and a deterrent to his child. Moreover, this allows many baby daddies to see the obligation to both the child and mother as difficult and even hate filled. This distorted mentality cannot sustain the father's involvement, as it is not conducive or nurturing for either the child or mother. This is especially evident after the dreams and aspirations of the baby's mother are pushed away and replaced with the daily pressures of sole child care.

This is the internal frustration that is widely known but reluctantly discussed in the African-American community. It is the true essence of what over 70% of single-parent, African American house holds live with daily. Everybody knows someone that has been invaded by a baby daddy and, in some cases, even by a baby mama. It has now become all too easy to watch potentially-forming African-American families painfully spiral and end in the most divisive manner of separation. This is brought about by either the irresponsible decisions of parents, who are not mature enough to deal with the consequences of sex, or by the law that grants many rights to the invasive and often elusive baby daddy.

5
How the law can give a "baby daddy" control over a marriage

Another scenario exists, which explains the invasion of the baby daddy throughout the African-American culture. This invasion tactic is when the baby daddy demands the right to see his child by using the law to interrupt the life of the mother. Out of spite, he uses the court to gain access to the mother and her new husband or boyfriend. This action can prevent the mother, child and new husband from leaving the state, if joint custody is established. Believe me, if I had not seen this law enforced first hand, I would have never believed it. It is so idiotic that the law can give a baby daddy more authority in a relationship--even a marriage, after the mother has "moved on" with her life. How can an uninvolved baby daddy, who never provided shelter, any child responsibility or even a promise of marriage, have this much influence?

Ironically, I am writing about my experiences, with no malice intended, yet I wish to highlight the unbelievable truth.

One question I ask myself everyday is, "How can a baby daddy obtain such high authority in a woman's life, even to the point where he can be allowed sole custody of a child?"

Unfortunately, this happens all too often, especially to women who take the law for granted by automatically thinking the court will provide them with custody (as the mother has historically served as the primary provider for the child). In my case, Rachel and I were not married when she took her baby daddy to court to file for child support. In the end, her baby daddy wanted revenge (by not wanting to pay the maximum for child support). He also went to court and established paternity rights to the child and falsified his financial reporting. Consequently, this led to a court date between both mother and father.

In many African American communities, the mother serves as the primary caregiver to the child. Many women take this for granted, as did Rachel. She believed that she would instantly win the case against her baby daddy, and that he would not get custody of their son. This attitude is indicative of many women in regards to custody and/or child support cases. In another instance, Rachel knew a single mother, who established court-sanctioned child support, without a lawyer. This left Rachel with a myopic viewpoint, in terms of how child support cases can rule, in favor of the mother. It is easy to see how women can be deceived by ignorance of the law and hearsay. Actually, it is rather expensive to traverse through the justice system with a custody case. It can normally average between eight and ten thousand dollars. Moreover, many women who are involved in custody cases, especially African-Americans with low socioeconomic status, can be financially taken through the ringer. The baby daddy may be financially challenged too, or in some cases be in a better financial situation than the mother. The complexity continues if the baby daddy can present himself with a lawyer, and the mother cannot. An attorney can present the baby daddy in ways that does not reflect his true character. This, unfortunately, distorts the mother's attributes to her child because in the eyes of the law, victory is granted the better proof of documentation.

As Rachel and I were not married at the time, I could not formally assist in the fight against her baby daddy. He happened to have a very reputable attorney, while she foolishly represented herself. It is common knowledge that when representing yourself as a client, you significantly increase the probability of an unfavorable verdict. Unfortunately, a mother's court loss can be catastrophic because it can ultimately result in the loss of sole custody, while simultaneously providing the baby daddy with a custody advantage.

As Rachel represented herself, her testimony, although true, was not taken seriously. Because she was facing a formidable opponent (i.e., an accomplished attorney), her testimony was invalidated, as he portrayed her as an unstable mother. Arguments may often occur between single mothers and their "sperm-donating" baby daddies. As the baby daddy provides very little help (or completely abandons both the child and mother), the mother is usually forced to provide sole responsibility. Depending on the severity of the situation, police involvement may occur when child visitation becomes an issue. In another case, that we were privileged to, both the mother and baby daddy warranted police involvement when the mother was documented for exuding belligerent behavior. According to the officer's statement, the mother was cursing and displayed the behavior of a "straight hood, sister-girl." It was not reported that the baby daddy was withholding the baby from his mother, while threatening the non-return of the child. Perhaps a situation like this would provoke erratic behavior from any caring parent.

Nonetheless, in the eyes of the court, as Rachel was without legal representation, the burden of proof to demonstrate her ability as a fit mother, resided with her. The baby daddy's attorney presented a series of boldface lies; such as: the sole provision of shelter for his child. As this never really happened, the attorney continually presented untruths to the court. The ultimate lie came when he fabricated the story of Rachel's decision to move out and decline the receipt of care for his child. Rachel refuted this claim, as the truth of the matter was that the baby daddy moved from the home that he and Rachel occupied. He then informed Rachel that the home was up for sale. He demanded that both she and their unborn child find a new place to live. After Rachel's delivery, she moved into her own apartment, where she has lived since.

Rachel stated that the birthday party for her child was attended by the baby daddy's parents. As the party was in Charlotte, the baby daddy reported that the party happened in South Carolina. According to Rachel, she had to reimburse the baby daddy's family for food that was brought for the celebration. It is noted that the two families possess a bitter history. Raw emotions continued to escalate with false allegations that Rachel denied her baby daddy visitation rights to his child.

In the end, the baby daddy received the winning verdict by being awarded permanent joint custody. This basically meant that Rachel could not have sole custody, although she was already the primary caregiver. The baby daddy had now been given the same legal authority for their child. This judgment forever crippled her ability to "move on" with her life, unless the judgment could be overturned through the appeals' process. Simultaneously, this solidified the permanent, lawful invasion of a baby daddy into Rachel's life. This judgment had severe ramifications. Situations of this magnitude significantly impact women across our country, on a daily basis. Hereto with, post the rendering of the verdict, she could no longer make any major decisions for her child, without the approval of her baby daddy. Moreover, practically every major decision involving the child, up to and including the place of residence, had to be approved by him. The child could not move anywhere without baby daddy consent. The school and healthcare provider had to follow the same protocol for approval. Ultimately, by far, the biggest compromise included the traveling plans of the mother, with her own child. In order for this to happen, written approval by the baby daddy had to be given, especially if the trip/absence was for an extended amount of time that may have interfered with his "court approved" time.

Now that I have spoken about how a baby mother could lose custody, let me also state that according to public record, the baby daddy actually had a DNA test conducted to prove his paternity. Rachel found this out one day before her court date. This information was not helpful, as she did not have legal representation to prove the baby daddy's initial denial of paternity. I could tell this deeply bothered her and with the court ruling, her life was forever changed.

It is a sad situation that happens all too often in the lives of unsuspecting people who may never prove to be aware of this type of crisis. This interferes with the way the mother can parent her child and may even prevent her from potentially forming a productive life, elsewhere. This legal baby-daddy invasion allowed the father to object to the potential residence for both the baby mother and their child, along with the new husband-to-be. The court mandate provided the baby daddy the authority to stop the mother from moving out of state, or even to another in-state location. Normally, a baby daddy is mandated by the state to pay child support. In Rachel's case, the court order negated this by granting permanent joint custody. As a result, the baby daddy was provided with as much authority to his child, as a married man has to his own children. In fact, the law almost marries the baby mother and daddy with respect to the welfare of the child. This is done as a result to promote maturity in working together for the common good. It is almost the most invasive situation any woman could ever experience.

The following is a caption of the actual court ruling from the State of North Carolina, in Mecklenburg County. This is public

46

information; therefore, no character defamation claims can be warranted:

STATE OF NORTH CAROLINA COUNTY OF MECKLINGBURG IN THE GENERAL COURT OF JUSTICE DISTRICT COURT DIVISION 04 CVD20559 JVH OCTOBER 17, 2005   PERMANENT CUSTODY ORDER
Evan Chambers, PLAINTIFF
VS.
Rachel Johnson, DEFENDANT

This matter came on for hearing on October 7, 2005 before the undersigned judge of family court for Mecklenburg County, North Carolina.   Present were the parties, with father represented by an attorney and mother representing herself.   Based on the evidence presented, matters of record and applicable law, the court makes the following:

FINDINGS OF FACT

1. The parties, both residents of Mecklenburg County, North Carolina, are the parents of a son, born April 9, 2003. The parties and their son have resided in Mecklenburg County for all pertinent periods.

2. Both parties filed claims for custody of their son.   Mother's counterclaim includes a claim for child support, but as there is another child support case between the parties, this claim will be dismissed.

3. The parties lived together before their son's birth and for a period of time thereafter.   Both were excited about having a child.   Father attended pregnancy classes with mother, participated in buying things for the baby and was present for his birth, taking pictures.   Both parents took time off from work several weeks after the baby's birth.

4. At some point before December 2003 the parties separated. Mother and child moved out of father's house in the UNCC area and into her own place. For a time, father saw the baby often, but by Christmas the situation changed. Mother was less willing to permit father to see the child, and father would go to child's daycare and see him there. The change was a result of reconciliation efforts failing.

5. Father was allowed on child's first birthday, to take him to a large family party in South Carolina.   Over the next year, however, the

47

party's relationship continued to deteriorate, and first agreeing in writing to allow father to take child for a family party on his second birthday, mother withdrew her agreement, kept the child from daycare so the father could not get him, and the child missed the party. Members of father's family who attended the party brought gifts for child but were told to take the gifts to their own grandchildren, so child missed the gifts as well as the party in his honor, and the chance to be with relatives.

6. The written agreement allowing father to take the child to his birthday party was signed in the presence of Officer Henry of CMPD, who was called because of the party's dispute, and who spoke with both parties. He found father to be calm and reasonable. He found mother to be belligerent, vulgar and profane. Officer Henry was concerned about the mother's behavior and language in the presence of the child. Mother and a female friend said father had assaulted mother, but Officer Henry did not find probable cause and made no report. When father later told him that the mother had withdrawn from their agreement, Officer Henry tried calling her twice, but mother did not return his calls.

7. The incident of child's second birthday is not an isolated example of mother denying father access to his child, with no valid reason. On other occasions as well, she has agreed for child to go with his father, then withdrawn her consent and refused to communicate with father. She uses the child as a pawn in the party's conflict. Without court order, the father has limited recourse.

8. Mother has also withheld information about child's medical treatment from father, in particular, not telling him about minor surgery child had because father had disagreed with her plan to have the surgery done.

9. On the positive side, both parents describe each other as "good" or "great" parents, and the evidence about their parenting, except for mother's arbitrary treatment of father, is all good.

CONCLUSION OF LAW

1. North Carolina has jurisdiction over the parties, the child, and the subject matter of this action.

2. The parties are fit and proper to share joint custody of their son, and this order is in the child's best interest. Based on the above

48

findings and conclusions, **it is herby ordered adjudged and decreed**:

1. **Permanent joint custody is awarded to the parties herein. Joint legal custody is defined as equal authority to make major decisions concerning their child's education, healthcare and religious upbringing.** The parents must confer, share information, and make these decisions together, with neither parent having the authority to override the other. If they reach an impasse, they must reenter child custody mediation to resolve it. Day-to-day decisions shall be made by the parent child is with at that time.

2. Child shall reside primarily with his mother and spend time with his father as the parties may agree. If they do not agree, father's time with Child shall be as follows:

a. alternate weekends, from 6 p.m. Friday until 6 p.m. Sunday

b. two overnight stays/week, which shall be Tuesday and Thursday, unless agreed otherwise, with father picking Child up from daycare to returning him to daycare the following morning.

c .all day (if the day is on a weekend) and overnight on Child's birthday in alternate, even numbered years for the Saturday following his birthday from 9 a.m. until 9 a.m. Sunday if the weekend is not father's regular weekend.

d. on Father's day each year, 9 a.m.-6 p.m. if it is not his regular weekend (similarly, mother shall have the child on Mother's day beginning at 9 a.m. if it is not her regular weekend).

e. Thanksgiving holidays from 6 p.m. Wednesday until 6 p.m. Sunday in 2005 and other odd-numbered years

f. when he begins school, all of spring vacation in even-number years, from 6 p.m. (the day school lets out) until 6 p.m. the day before it resumes.

g. in odd-numbered years, from 2 p.m. on December 25 until 6 p.m. the day before school resumes; in even-number years, from 6 p.m. the day school lets out for Christmas holidays until 2 p.m. on December 25.

h. in 2006 and 2007 for one week's summer vacation, the week to be chosen by May 1; in 2008 and thereafter for two weeks' summer vacation, chosen by May 1.

3. Mother may also choose a vacation week for the summers of 2006 and 2007 and two vacation weeks for 2008 and thereafter, by May 10 each year.

4. Holiday and summer visits/vacation time shall supersede the regular schedule.

5. Both parties shall have equal access to all records concerning their child, equal access to all facilities where the child may be, and equal rights to participate in functions such as parent-teacher conferences, medical appointments and extracurricular activities.

6. The parents shall share information concerning their son with each other. Each shall keep the other informed of any changes in address, telephone or email. Both shall promptly return calls/letters from the other.

7. Child may freely call one parent when with his other parent. Each parent may call Child at reasonable times when he is with his other parent. Calls shall be promptly returned.

8. Both parents shall treat each other with civility and respect at all times and insist that others do the same.

This 17th day of October, 2005
Barbara Culter, Judge Presiding
Cc Gloria Devine Attorney
Rachel Johnson

As seen in its entirety, the current order displays the appearance of favoritism in respect to the baby's father. It further emphasizes the point that the law can be used to manipulate rights of invasion for the baby daddy. My personal advice to any male or female, who may find themselves going to court to fight a baby daddy or mother, would be to never go without legal representation.

This order was in place a year before Rachel and I got married. It could only be changed, if she presented just cause that a substantial change in her life would require her to move out of state. I was unaware of this through the first year of our marriage.

In reminiscing about my marriage to Rachel, I can honestly say that the entire day was wonderful. We were married in Georgia, and I will never forget the scene of the church that was full of well wishers and plenty of family. I felt full of joy and confident that this was the best move of my life, as there was no limitation to the love in my heart. Rachel's son was very happy with our union. His smiles of joy radiated throughout the plenty of pictures that were taken. Our day was full of dancing and good times, and Rachel was beautiful. She was dressed in a beautiful, white wedding gown with a small train and a lovely veil. Rachel's beautiful smile and natural brown eyes lit up the altar of the church. My heart burst with tears as she walked down the aisle, escorted by her uncle. In the happiest day of my life, we establish our souls, under the blessings of an Almighty God, in the presence of family and friends whom we both loved dearly. I was, without a doubt, on top of the world that day.

I assumed that the baby daddy only had visitation with his son. Neither she nor I really knew the legal extent of the order that gave the baby daddy control throughout our marriage, just because he had a child with my wife. This order trapped Rachel to her baby daddy. It also hindered Rachel from marriage, as it practically prevented her from moving on with a new husband by using the child as handcuffs.

I cannot tell you how difficult it is to maintain a marriage with a baby daddy who possessed a certain amount of control over my wife. Instead of having my wife in the same city with me, she remained in Charlotte. It is the greatest strain on a marriage when a spouse's past is unfinished; resulting in a hindrance on the future. No one envisions a marriage in this way, as this creates division, mistrust and humiliation. I may be a little selfish; however, the spouse is the true victim in a situation like this. He or she remains helpless, outside of the two parents bonded by the child. A woman or a man with shared custody of a child from a previous relationship compromises future life decisions. Many, in the African-American community, generally steer clear of this kind of relationship. This is because of the belief that both the baby daddy and mother will always have some form of emotional bond and a "revolving-door" option for sex with each other. This generally impacts young, failed relationships, as both are unable to get along, but cannot rid themselves of the sexual desires for each other. Most importantly, there is a disconnect to the responsibility of the child.

In my case, the past intimacy was not the problem, nor the threat of any remaining sexual desire. It was merely the idea of

Rachel being caught between wanting to move on with her new husband, and a court order that retained her, by virtue of her child, to a reluctant baby daddy. It was a real shame that the law did not give Rachel an opportunity to move on with her life. African-American families have a barrier to overcome when it comes to understanding the law. Policy keeps the family separated and can thwart responsibility in either direction. I personally believe that any man who has a child should take care of his responsibility. All children born out of wedlock are innocent. They are just as much a victim (if not more) in the tug-of-war between the mother and father. This is often challenging for children to deal with because they are used as a "bargaining chip" in the relationship, or lack thereof. Forever has life-long implications and when the shock is over that the person really is not who you thought they were, anger and bitterness builds quickly. Before long, reality sets in like a burning flame in the furnace of life. Hatred takes root and guilt soon follows.

I observed my wife expressing great sorrow on how she had a son with a man whom she once loved. She even provided their offspring with his name. I talked to Rachel about the demise of their relationship. She expressed her feelings of betrayal and how she lost confidence in her baby daddy. She realized that he was not the man, she once loved. Unfortunately, she became pregnant during her epiphany. I can only imagine the disappointment she must have felt, and I know that Rachel still regrets this today. Not her son, but the man who fathered her child and devastated her life. She learned shortly after our marriage that she was under court order, with permanent joint custody to her baby daddy.

My wife was beat down by the legal system. She believed that she had been railroaded. While feeling guilty for not hiring an attorney, she had only herself to blame for the court's verdict. As we were in a real quagmire, we tried desperately to hold on to our marriage. In the meantime, I was in Tennessee developing my medical practice. Despite the odds, I held on to my marriage as best I could.

I was married on paper and wore a ring, but I would often go places, even to church by myself. The following years of my marriage consisted of numerous flights to see my wife and her son.

As I did my best to make our marriage work, it became easier to entertain the idea of separation. I was extremely lonely, yet I had a reputation of being a "good man" to uphold. I did not want to sacrifice my integrity or people's perceptions of me, as it would have been "second nature" for me to become a player. Instead, I continued to pursue my marriage. I held on in the hopes that Rachel and her baby daddy would come to some sort of truce.

My marriage was worthless in comparison to the blood of another man's child.

As a man, I felt psychologically robbed of something that I waited 35 years to find. I even felt that somehow I had forfeited a good selection for a wife. Perhaps I had brought this on myself. Nonetheless, I continually prayed for resolve and mercy. I found myself constantly asking God to lighten my load, as I would not wish this situation on any man. With authority, I can state that if you are considering marrying a woman with kids think twice, as you may never know how deep the well of a woman's heart may go.

As a man and husband, my voice was muted by the family court because all court orders rule in the best interest of the child. For women, I think that it is much easier to find a "good guy" because a separated/divorced man usually does not have custody of his kids. If a woman establishes a relationship with this kind of man, it becomes challenging for her to be second to the baby mama. This is especially true when she (i.e., baby mama) uses tactics of keeping the daddy mentally strapped by court proceedings or child support.

All of this information was shared with me in the attorney's office in North Carolina. It felt as if someone had ripped the foundation of life right from under my feet. I found myself instantly angry with my wife, as I felt deceived. My initial thought was that I had been duped into marrying her. Frustrated, confused and angry, I could see that Rachel was beginning to cry. My finding out about the court order really broke her down. My realization was that throughout our marriage, her baby daddy had more control than I did.

The attorney we sought counsel from told me that we were already facing an uphill battle at this point. He said that I could not take my family out of North Carolina, because the order had given the baby daddy joint custody. Generally, we would like to think that no mother would leave her child to have a marriage. God knew that I did not want to ask my wife to do that. Therefore, the baby daddy had ultimate control, while I remained helpless. Ironically, the law gave him this power, as he never wanted to assume it naturally through marriage. At that point, I could never imagine that a baby daddy could legally hold a child and mother hostage, while being granted the convenience to invade the woman's marriage at will. This act alone should evidently show the immaturity of Rachel's baby daddy, and his ambition to avoid the best interests of his child.

All child development experts agree that small children are usually better served by being raised by the mother, when marriage is nonexistent. Moreover, it stands to reason that the baby daddy did not take this into consideration at all. Perhaps, in his mind, having his child taken from the mother to avoid paying child support was his way of "getting back" at her for moving on with her life. It may have also served as a means of control. Regardless, the court saw everything from his point of view. I am certain that Rachel did not know what the implications of her case would be. I have continually repeated this for my own sanity. As hindsight is always 20/20, I have accepted the logical conclusion that she would have, otherwise, chosen legal counsel, if she could have magically re-lived her court date.

Although this order was placed over Rachel and her child, it interfered with my wishes for a life of marital convenience. This compromise became painfully apparent when Rachel could not travel with me, as a result of her child being unable to leave the state. We were especially inconvenienced whenever provisions had to be made for either baby daddy visitation and/or overnight stays. Quite naturally, tensions grew between us, as we would constantly argue over how stupid she was for going to court without an attorney.

6

When baby daddies are around like a Phantom

I could tell that our marriage was really going through a tough challenge when my wife and I began to argue and stay intensely frustrated. The worst part of everything was that I could do nothing to help. At first, I flew in on weekends and tried not to think about divorce, but the more I flew, the more I began to entertain the thought. I thought that by divorcing Rachel, I would be out of the way. This would have allowed her to concentrate on being a single mother and deal with her baby daddy, for the rest of her life. However, my wife and I had already been married for two years and no matter what a person says, it is hard to walk away when you really love someone. Even if you feel that you are not at fault and have been deceived by love.

It would have been hard to leave Rachel and annul the marriage, because I really wanted this. This was the first time in my life that I had committed to building something, such as: my medical practice, a relationship and raising children. Besides, it was not like Rachel and I hated one another's guts, it was simply that her situation with the court order was difficult to get around. I realized that if I left Rachel and my new step son that I would be walking out on a woman that really loved me as a person. When you can see a little light at the end of a tunnel, you put in all of your energy, in the hopes that your reward will be well deserved. If you can get through the maze of heartbreak and disappointment, then do what you've got to do—life is too short.

With all of the challenges that could have come with the situation of being away from my wife, she and I had some personal failures at procreation. It gives me no pleasure to talk about how stress broke down the physical and mental conditioning of our relationship. Moreover, I was completely unhappy with our living arrangement of touch and go. We were married with no intimacy, on a daily basis. On the surface, we worked to appear delightful but deep inside, a feeling of agony and loneliness prevailed in my heart.

I can distinctly remember when I visited my wife in North Carolina, in August of 2007. That night, we had a reasonable evening and went to bed.

As it was early in the morning, about 3:00 am, Rachel woke me up and said in a scared voice, "Mark, wake up. I don't feel good. I'm hurtin' really bad!"

I asked, "Rachel, what did you eat tonight? Do you think it's gas? Did you try to go to the bathroom?"

"I can't go to the bathroom! I feel pain when I stand and sit down on the toilet...My stomach feels tight...Ahh!"

I knew that she was in a lot of pain, so I jumped out of bed and touched Rachel's stomach. I observed that it was very tight and warm. As I began to think of everything that it could be, I figured that it was probably appendicitis.

I asked Rachel, "Baby, where are you hurting? How often does it hurt?"

"It's in my lower stomach, just above my vagina...Oh my God! It really hurts, Mark!"

As her pain worsened, my medical training helped me to narrow this down to complications of pregnancy, appendicitis or even pelvic inflammatory disease.

I asked Rachel, "Do you have any pain medication in the house?"

"It's so old that I don't want to take it. I have some Motrin in the cabinet. It's really hurtin'. Can I just lie down and try to sleep it off? I'm tired."

The bells began to go off, as I realized that I was dealing with a medical emergency. Rachel was losing consciousness rapidly and getting weaker. As her pain was rapidly increasing, I got her son dressed and placed Rachel in the car. We hurriedly drove to the Carolina medical center hospital in Charlotte.

As we were driving, Rachel shouted, "Mark, please be careful going over the bumps in the damn road! When you hit 'em, I can feel the pain in my stomach!"

I replied calmly, "I'm sorry baby. I'm just trying to get you to the emergency room as fast as I can."

I felt Rachel's lower abdominal area, and it felt distended and warm. This was not good. On this scary night, my fear of the inevitable was gradually becoming a reality. All I could do was pray and ask God to let me get her to the emergency room safely, before she became worse or lost consciousness.

I knew that this was something very serious. Although I was hopeful that she was pregnant; all-in-all, I knew that whatever it was; it required medical attention and fast. We finally arrived at the hospital and I parked close to the emergency room, so that Rachel would not have far to go.

I ran to the ER, got a wheel chair, and wheeled Rachel into the emergency area. As I entered the ER, I began to shout, "Hey, please, can someone evaluate my wife? She's in a lot of pain!"

The receptionist asked me, "Do you know when the pain started and how often it's occurring? Is she pregnant?"

I replied, "The pain started early this morning, about half an hour ago. It's gotten worse since then and her stomach is distended and warm to hot to the touch."

At this time, Rachel placed her head in her hands and suddenly began to vomit and scream. The nurses hurriedly responded by evaluating her. A medical stability team responded, as it seemed that everyone understood the emergency, at that moment.

My step son asked worriedly, "Daddy Mark, will my mama be all right? I hope she stop hurtin'."

I tried to reassure him that she would be okay, but I did not know myself.

I replied, "Well, mommy is going to be okay. The doctors and nurses are taking care of her and we'll see her soon. Don't worry, mommy is strong and she won't be in pain for long."

I could see in his little face that he was just as scared and worried as I was. He sat in my lap as we sat in silence and hoped for the best. I prayed silently. The nurses took Rachel into a room, where she was able to lay in a hospital bed. They took a urine sample and some blood. An IV was inserted into her arm.

Rachel asked, "Can y'all please give me something for the pain!"

A nurse replied, "Rachel, the doctor is on his way. We'll be able to give you something in a second when we find out if you're pregnant or not. Just bear with us for a second."

The nurses were very courteous to us. Pregnancy was a real

eye opener for the both of us, as we had not been that sexually active. We were using condoms for a while, until a few months ago. I never told Rachel but during sex, I would take it off. I had also gotten comfortable with not pulling out. This happened a few times earlier that month, as I was ready to have a child.

The nurse returned and said, "Well, we're pregnant, but I have both good and bad news. Because the baby is in the fallopian tubes and not in the uterus, I'm sorry to tell you that…"

I quickly interjected, "Will Rachel be all right?"

The nurse said, "I don't know…we'll have to let her doctor tell you the rest."

The doctor returned after the ultrasound reading and said, "We will have to get your wife to surgery right away because she has an ectopic pregnancy. She is bleeding internally from her uterine artery rupture."

I was surprised and grateful because we were pregnant. The feeling quickly fled, as fast as it came. In the next moment, my soaring spirit fell to the ground because the wonderful surprise pregnancy had now become a surgical emergency, with two lives hanging in the balance. Consequently, my wife was attempting to hold onto a developing embryo that was dying in her left fallopian tube. I may not be able tell you how it feels to lose a child, but I can tell you that when a pregnancy you have waited on, for over 35 years, is severely compromised, it feels like an impending train wreck, where you know somebody is going to die. Just as I suspected, we lost our child. Rachel almost died in the process. She had to have two blood transfusions to restore her total blood volume, as she was hospitalized for four days in the Carolina Medical Center.

Another unfortunate incident began with my wife missing her period for a few months. She was very excited but was also dealing with a lot of stress. As a result, my wife made a trip to see me. She flew from Charlotte to Memphis.

She claimed, after the plane ride, that she had a very painful feeling in her lower back.

She stated, "Mark, I feel like lying down, my back is hurting…I really don't feel good."

I knew something was wrong, but once again I tried to remain positive and not think about my wife having a natural miscarriage. Over that weekend, I watched my wife like a hawk. Her condition slightly improved. As I could not rest, my wife's positive pregnancy test provided a much needed relief.

After that weekend, Rachel flew back to Charlotte. I advised her to go to the hospital for a check up to see if the pregnancy was still a viable situation. Although hopeful, I remained skeptical of our successful pregnancy. I never stopped praying to God for mercy. The nurse took some blood and tested the human chorionic growth hormone (HCG). During pregnancy, the woman's body produces this hormone for the growth and development of the fetus. Her HCG levels were actually 678.

The nurse asked my wife, "How many weeks are you along?"

Rachel replied, "At least 3-4 weeks since my last menstrual cycle...I'm sure of that."

The nurse told my wife that she should return the following week to check the HCG levels. She also recommended that she see her OBGyn. My wife called me that night, and we talked about it. We talked about her hospital visit, and I reassured her that I would be there no matter the outcome. The following week, my wife returned to the hospital to have more blood drawn. This time, her HCG levels were 486. The nurse advised my wife that she may be experiencing a miscarriage, but she was unsure.

She instructed, "Rachel, your HCG numbers are supposed to double over a week...yours are beginning to drop. We'll follow up next week and see where we are. I don't want you to worry right now, okay."

This information proved to be a psychological blow to both my wife and I. As we equally wanted this baby, we both knew of the looming horrors of pregnancy failure. I could feel my wife's frustration change to worry, fear and even guilt of what may be on the horizon. Although we did not speak it, somehow, we knew that we would have to face another loss. The following week, my wife and I went to the hospital together for another blood draw and ultrasound. This time, her HCG level was 346.

The nurse said, "I am going to have the doctor talk to you both about the findings and what you'll need to do from here."

I replied, "Does it seem that the pregnancy has failed?"

The nurse replied, "The doctor will let you know the results and what they mean today."

I looked at my wife's face and saw the tears developing. It was then that the sadness and the anguish of a miscarriage became all too real. We both felt the impending death of our unborn child, in the immediate future. Both of us began to cry and hold on to one another. The doctor came into the room with a great bedside manner.

He stated, "It seems that we have an unfortunate circumstance of miscarriage presently occurring. When the HCG levels continue to drop, as in your case, it means that the embryo is not viable, and the pregnancy has naturally begun to abort. This is the body's natural process of ending a pregnancy that will not develop full term. You may also experience some cramping and soon you'll feel something similar to a menstrual period occur. That will most likely be the tissue of the embryo being removed from the uterus by the natural process of miscarriage. I am very sorry, but you are still a young couple. After all things clear up, you can always try again."

I thanked the doctor, as my wife and I left the hospital knowing that death had again won this round. This was taking a toll on Rachel, as she felt like a failure. I could not understand how the baby daddy had no problem with having his child with Rachel, while I was having so much difficulty. Things were now going horribly wrong in my marriage. Life can be ironic at times. Its cruelty can make one question God of His will. As it goes from bad to worse for the "good guys," the baby daddy always seems to remain unphased. My anxiety peeked as I began to realize that I was not going to be as successful as the baby daddy was, in conceiving a child with my wife. This series of events made me feel like I was less than a man. Even worse, I felt like I had married damaged goods, after the elusive baby daddy had wrecked my chances for a family with my wife, but always his baby mama.

Just as the doctor told us what would happen, Rachel began to have heavy menstrual periods. Heavy clumps of bloody embryonic debris fell into the toilet when my wife would go to the bathroom. This was due to the pressure of these heavy cycles of substance coming out of her vagina. I actually saw the clumps of bloody tissue in the toilet. I felt defeated as a man because I knew that this was a part of my anatomy, my DNA, lying in the toilet. At one point, I actually reached in the toilet, picked it up and observed the bloody clump. I cried as I came to the horrid realization of defeat. It hurt badly, because I needed to have this family. I needed to feel complete. I began to question my own manhood, as I did not believe that I was man enough to have a successful pregnancy. Ultimately, I descended into depression.

I thanked God, at least a thousand times, that I did not live in Charlotte. This would have consistently and persistently reminded me of the tragedy that was my marriage. I was grateful that I had my medical practice in Tennessee, as this was home for me. This kept my mind occupied and off the loss of the pregnancy. It also preserved my hopes of a better situation that could possibly come with time.

I would often go to church and pray. I would ask God why I was suffering and what had I done to deserve a marriage like this. I never dreamed that it would turn out so horrible for me, and the circumstances would be more than I could bear. It was then that I found myself praying to God for comfort and soul satisfaction. I felt good every time I went to church at the Temple of Deliverance (COGIC) in Memphis, TN. The late, great Bishop G.E. Patterson founded this church March 6, 1975. Although he died in 2007, his legacy still carries on. Superintendent Milton R. Hawkins is now the pastor, and he has a great message that is really "soul stirring." God uses him to minister the Word to the hearts and minds who have need of encouragement. He is certainly carrying on the legacy of his late uncle, Bishop G.E. Patterson. I have been a member, since 1999 and have always felt the spirit move me, as I prayed to God in the temple. I often asked God to allow me to raise a family in this church and have the whole community Christian experience.

It came to pass that Rachel and I began to feel the invasion, as a result of the court order, so we went to see an attorney to investigate the option of getting it changed. The attorney told both of us that Rachel was in a real mess and that we would be fighting an "uphill battle." The attorney pointed out to us that Rachel made her first mistake by trying to represent herself in court. Although Rachel was beginning to cry, I knew that she was dealing with some critical, emotional memories. This was compounded by the resounding tone of her mother, who told her that she should have gotten an attorney the first time.

The attorney's visit cost me $1,500.00 to retain his services. I was not frustrated over the money. I was; however, more frustrated over how I was just finding out, after two years of marriage, that I had been invaded. I felt deceived, hurt and even used by Rachel. Why didn't she tell me about the court order, before we were married?

I asked, "How in the hell did you get yourself in to this? Don't you know that you never go to court without an attorney? What's wrong with you?"

Rachel replied, "I didn't have the money, and I didn't think I needed one to get this done. I didn't think that it would turn out like this."

We stormed out of the attorney's office, as I barked at Rachel, "You know, you ain't worth this shit! Why can't you get it together?"

Rachel had tears in her eyes, "Mark, I don't want to lose you...I'm sorry. I swear I didn't know that it was going to be like this. I'm so sorry I didn't tell you about the order, but I didn't understand how hard it would hit us. I swear, Mark...please believe me!"

I did not totally buy her story, and I never saw my wife the same way from that day forward. I lost something for Rachel, right then and there. It had now become evident that this was the beginning of the end. Despite my anger, I wanted the marriage to be over, but when love is involved, your feelings of anger and hurt can cloud your judgment. You still have to consider that your heart has a space reserved for the good, the bad and the ugly of a person. As I was vulnerable, my judgment remained compromised. These feelings can cause you to stay with a person, even when deep inside, you just want to get the hell out.

Consequently, I remained married and tried to make the best of it. It was painful because I knew that the baby daddy still had a relationship with his son, while living his life free of any drama. I was the victim holding the result of his past, as he invaded my life and dictated my actions. I hated being in this situation. It was as if there was a phantom in my marriage, as he took control of both my life and happiness. This "phantom menace" added stress and agony that seemed to kill my marriage daily.

7
When marriage is tested what do you do?

The attorney set the trial date for October 13, 2008. It was here that we began our battle to reverse the impending "baby daddy" court order. As that date did not manifest, the court reset the trial date for November 4, 2008. When the court postponed that date, I began feeling like the order would never have a chance of being removed. In the meantime, Rachel continued dropping off her son, while the baby daddy continued his rein.

Finally, in February 2009, it seemed that we had some luck with changing the existing order; unfortunately, the court could not lock the judge in time to hear the case. As a result, the date was reset for March 27, 2009. This time, we finally locked in the judge. It took a total of 6 months, from October 2008 to March of 2009, to have our case heard. Moreover, it was embarrassing to see how my life was totally turned upside down in the process. We were arguing more frequently over the smallest things. Tensions were unbearable, as our marriage continued to unravel. Rachel noticed that I did not want intimacy anymore. I knew that she could feel my disappointment, knowing that I did not ask to be in this situation. My assessment yielded even more pain, upon realizing that she was never really my wife or my girl. In my mind, she was, and had always been, the custody of another man.

As I was still angry with Rachel for her lack of "baby daddy" disclosure, I was still hoping that a revised court order could help save our marriage. I really prayed that God would help me to forgive my wife. This would contribute 50 percent to the resolve of our marriage. Forgiveness would be completely necessary if we were going to make it through this difficult time.

Finally, the trial started at the Mecklenburg County Court house in Charlotte, N.C. I was a little nervous, although I was not the one on trial. Through it all, I was there to support my wife. Our months of marital tension had come down to this very moment. Eventually, I knew that if we did not get the old order changed, we would be at the end of what we were trying to hold on to. As the stakes were high, somehow, we knew that there was a slim chance for success.

The trial day began and all parties came to the court room. Witnesses sat in their respective places, ready to demonstrate their support. My wife's mother sat next to me with her friend and sister. Seeing the baby daddy in court was a reminder of the phantom-figure in my marriage. It was a real shame to see how the situation had become a reality drama. The irony was that I was heavily involved in a situation of this caliber, while simultaneously being as helpless as a newborn. I saw the opposing party's family enter the court room. They took their seats on the baby daddy's side of the court room.

The judge entered the courtroom, as the bailiff commanded, "All rise."

Almost immediately, the judge responded for us to be seated. The judge was a woman and seemed to be a great person of integrity and wisdom in family court cases. The attorneys introduced their cases to the courtroom. It seemed that the baby daddy was trying for complete custody of his child. This came as a surprise, as Rachel was attempting to do the same thing. Our attorney attempted to show just cause of why she should be allowed full custody. Afterwards, the judge advised for all testifying parties to leave the courtroom. This tactic is often times used in court to prevent the bias impact of testimony. Therefore, all of the family, including myself and others, had to leave the courtroom, and, one-by-one, people began testifying and presenting documents demonstrating that my wife was the most involved parent in raising her son. Most of the testimonies gave credibility to my wife and very little support to the baby daddy. Finally, it was my turn to take the stand and our hired attorney was first with the line of questioning.

He began by asking, "Dr. Sand, please state your name and legal state of residence for the court."

I replied, "My name is Dr. Mark A. Sand, and I currently live in Tennessee."

The attorney asked, "What do you do for a living?"

"I am a Family Physician and treat ailments that affect adults and kids. I have been in practice in Tennessee for the last 4 years."

The attorney continued, "What is your relationship to Mrs. Sand and how long have you known her?"

I replied, "I am the husband, and I have known my wife for, at least, 6 years. We have been married for three years."

"When did you meet your wife?"

I replied, "I met her on November 29, 2002."

The attorney followed up, "How long did you date before you decided to marry your wife?"

I answered, "My wife and I dated for about two years."

The attorney then posed an interesting question, "If your wife and her child are allowed to leave the state of North Carolina, will she have to work?"

I replied, "No, she would not have to work at all, and I will gladly take on her child to provide care for him. In fact, I have proposed a private school, Henly Academy, which would be a great school for him to attend."

The attorney continued his follow up, "Dr. Sand, tell the court what does your home have to offer your wife and her son that will be better than what they have in the state of North Carolina?"

"My home has 4 bed rooms, a media room, a library/study, full kitchen and great room, with a three-car garage complete with basketball and tennis courts on my property. I have a great church community and good neighborhoods, with private schools and good colleagues who are professionals in their respective fields."

The attorney followed, "Dr. Sand how did you meet the plaintiff?

I replied, "Yes, I met him briefly at my step son's second birthday party. We exchanged a few words in regards to school and some commonalities. He appeared to be a nice guy."

The attorney continued, "Dr. Sand, how does the child receive you in his life and who does the child refer to you as?"

"The child calls me 'Daddy Mark,' and we have a good relationship. I don't talk bad to him about his dad, and I always let him know that he has to respect his dad."

That was the end of questioning from my attorney, but the plaintiff's attorney took over and began with her line of questioning.

She asked, "Dr. Sand, how long have you been married?"

I replied, I have been married for three years, and I met my wife November 29, 2002."

She continued, "Dr. Sand, are you aware that your wife had an existing order with my client before she married you?"

I replied, "I was not aware of that order when I married her."

"Dr. Sand, would the knowledge of that order have changed your decision to marry?"

My attorney said sharply, "Objection, Dr. Sand is not on trial here."

The opposing attorney stated, "Well, he should be able to tell the court how he feels about his marriage."

The judge responded, "Overruled. Dr. Sand can speak about everything pertaining to his marriage."

I thought for a brief moment and replied, "I trust my wife, and I am here to support her. I have taken on the responsibility of caring for her and her son. If allowed, I would love for us to be a family. That is why I am here today."

The opposing attorney asked, "Dr. Sand, when did you and your wife begin dating regularly?"

I replied, "We began dating pretty regularly in the fall of 2003. We kept in touch with each other after she had delivered her son. It was about 4 months after her delivery that things escalated to the level that we were becoming much more serious about our relationship."

She continued, "Did you know that your wife lived with my client all the way up to December of 2003, even after you guys began dating one another?"

I was a caught off guard with that question. After a minute, I quickly regained my composure and replied, "No, I was not aware of that."

Rachel later proved that this was not true in her testimony.

She continued, "Can you tell me what this reads on the order in the second paragraph?"

The second paragraph provided stipulations on both even and odd-numbered birthday weekends. The order stated that on the even number birthday weekend, the father is supposed to have the child, while on the odd-numbered birthday weekends, the mother of the child will have custody.

The opposing attorney asked, "Was the child with you in Tennessee, last year on his birthday, in 2008?"

"Yes, the child was with my wife and me on his birthday."

"Was that an odd or even year that the child was with you on that weekend?"

I thought for a second before answering, "Yes, that was an even year that he was with us."

The attorney stated, "Your honor, for the record, here is proof according to the second paragraph of the permanent joint custody court order evidence #17 that the child was not with the father according to the order as it is written."

The opposing attorney then asked me, "Dr. Sand, were you aware of this order and what it meant in regards to the custody of the father?"

I replied, "No, I had no previous knowledge that a court order existed, until a few months ago. I never knew about the child's agreement for certain birthdays or about any particular arrangement of time with the father."

"Dr. Sand, when did you know that you would be making Tennessee your permanent home?"

I replied, "I knew over 7 years ago that Tennessee would be my home. A good while before I even met my wife. I let her know that this is where I was going to set up my career. The connections I had there, really allowed me to get established in my practice."

The attorney then asked, "Dr. Sand, you mentioned that you have a great church and a good community to offer this child, but you can watch your church on T.V. as well. You are a member of the late G.E. Patterson's church in Tennessee? That is a big global church, so you can catch that church atmosphere here, in the state of North Carolina, right?"

I replied, "Church is not a spectator sort of thing. You must be a part of a community, with your family to experience the culture and enjoy church for what it is. I want to share that with my wife and her son. Wouldn't you want to have that with your family? I want to be a family and share these things like anybody else, if the court would allow me that opportunity."

"Dr. Sand, what will happen to your wife's son, if the state does not allow him to go with you and your wife?"

I replied, "The child will be sick without his mother, and my wife would be devastated."

The attorney continued, "From what you are trying to achieve, do you think that your removal of the child will have the same effect on my client? What is different between you and my client?"

I replied, "The difference is that I married my wife, and I took on both her life and the life of her child. He did not."

The opposing attorney tried to continue with her line of questioning, but the judge intervened and stated, "Dr. Sand has answered your questions fully and shown the difference between himself and the child's father. He is married to the defendant. If you have no further questions, Dr. Sand is free to leave the stand."

The attorney said, "No further questions for this witness."

The judge then replied, "Dr. Sand you may leave the stand now."

Shortly after my testimony, the judge called for a recess and ordered us to return at the end the day. The judge seemed like she wanted to end on that day. At one point, I thought that she was ready to reach a positive verdict, but the lawyers kept fighting over insignificant issues like: admission of photographs and the father's place of residence. As a result of the legal bickering, the judge stated that she would conclude all proceedings and reconvene on April 19th, for a second trial date.

I was devastated that the court proceedings did not end on the first day. For me, it really meant that we had to pay the attorney $4,200 more to try to case again. During this three-week period, our attorney was supposed to use this time to cover all facts and evidence that the opposing attorney could potentially use against us. However, due to our attorney's lack of professionalism and attention to detail, he did not follow through on his research. During this three-week period (i.e., March 27th through April 19th), our attorney did nothing for the advancement of our case. This shortfall would ultimately come back to haunt us and become the catalyst for the pivotal turn of events that could be best described as a tragedy.

Furthermore, the baby daddy taped some very heated conversations between himself and my wife. These moments were obviously in the recent history of the last court order. Those tapes would prove to be a crucial blow to our case, as our attorney had no rebuttal. As it turned out, a proper follow up showed that a letter of discovery was presented, during week 3 of our recess. Interrogatories had not been conducted.

On a personal note, my humble opinion is that if you ever have to get an attorney to fight a custody trial, get an attorney who is not lazy or works by himself. It may cost you a little more, but the outcome should be better since two or more heads work better than one. Get an attorney who has an assistant or a paralegal who acts as the firm's "arms and legs." They will also think with your attorney to cover the things that he or she may not have covered. The attorney we hired had been practicing since 1978, but he was an older, laidback white guy and seemingly had lost his keen attention to detail, regarding courtroom etiquette.

The opposing attorney operated in total contrast. She was an African-American female—younger and more charismatic with her articulation of the law. She was certainly more lawfully skillful, as she was well-researched on our case. She had a paralegal who worked with her on her cases and also accompanied her in court. I know she represented the baby daddy, but if I ever have any trouble in the state of North Carolina, I want her to represent me. To be fair, I can honestly say that she ran rings around our attorney. I thought she was excellent. However, not knowing how to choose an attorney or being inexperienced in these situations, money and affordability proved to be the overall factors for legal representation. I guess there's some truth to the saying, "You get what you pay for." Our defense's poor preparation eventually took its toll.

On April 19, 2009, the trial reconvened, and all parties once again entered the courtroom. My mother-in-law and I were both present.

My wife took the stand and placed her hand on the bible, as the bailiff asked, "Do you solemnly swear to tell the truth; the whole truth so help you God?"

"Yes, yes I do," replied Rachel.

Our attorney approached my wife and asked, "Could you state your name and why are you here in this courtroom today, for the court record?"

My wife replied, "My name is Rachel Sand, and I am here to

challenge the current order of joint custody.

Our attorney continued, "Have you made any attempts to change the agreement by working with the plaintiff, before the trial started?"

My wife replied, "Yes, I did through mediation of the court, but we could never work anything out."

"Has your husband supported you in this process and could you have done anything without his support?"

My wife answered, "Yes, and I could not afford to try this case without his help."

"How would you describe your marriage with Dr. Sand?"

My wife responded, "I feel that he is a great husband and gives great support to me and my life. I feel secure with him caring for my son and being there to help, even now, during this trial."

"Have you always known that Dr. Sand would be in Tennessee to start his career or is that something that you learned after you got to know him?"

My wife glanced up at the ceiling for a second to gather her thoughts.

She finally replied, "I knew that Mark was going to Tennessee, but he had also spoken about other places. I know that Tennessee was a big place that he mentioned that he was looking into."

Our attorney continued, "When did Dr. Sand let you know where he was going for sure?"

My wife replied, "He let me know for sure about a year or so before he graduated from his residency in New York."

"How would you describe the relationship between your son and Dr. Sand?"

"My son loves Mark, and they have a great relationship. He really looks up to him and they get along well."

"Has the son's father been involved as often as the court order has given him privilege to do so?"

My wife replied, "No, he has not been involved as he should have, nor has he kept up with weekday visits. He has missed some weekends and important school events also."

The opposing attorney shouted, "Objection! The council is

leading the witness in how to respond to the question."

The judge asserted, "Sustained. Counsel, you cannot lead the witness."

I could see that our attorney was getting a little frustrated in his line of questioning, as he continued examining my wife. It was becoming painfully obvious that our attorney was having a hard time examining my wife because she was not made aware of how to answer cross examining questions in court. Their preparation time was very little and it showed.

Our attorney continued, "Do you feel that the plaintiff loves his son?"

My wife replied, "I feel that he does love his son, but his son is obviously not his priority. His other women, his rental homes and his job are his priority, not his son."

Our attorney continued, "How do you feel that this order is preventing you from a life with your husband?"

The opposing attorney interjected, "Objection, your honor! The counsel is continuing to lead his witness!"

The judge agreed and said, "Sustained, counsel. We have talked about that already, and you know I cannot allow this form of cross examination in the court room."

The judge continued, "Ask your witness in another way to allow her to answer for herself, without you feeding her on how to answer. This is her life, and she should know how to answer her own affairs."

Our attorney sat back in his chair and took off his glasses with frustration all over his face.

He burst out, "Now, Rachel, this is your shot to tell the court how the plaintiff is affecting your life by this order!"

My wife replied, "This order is keeping me from my husband and a chance of having a family. I would love to be with my husband and raise our family in Tennessee. This order keeps my son from having a good, stable environment, while preventing us from marriage—one that I would love to keep."

Our attorney then rested with frustration and said, "No further questions for this witness."

I could clearly see his frustration and that he wanted to bring out more facts against the baby daddy. In that same vein, my wife was so nervous about the questions, while trying not to sound like a vicious, bitter, mad black woman, that she forgot to discuss the negative character of the baby daddy that the court needed to hear. Her testimony sounded empty, devoid of sincerity and passion. I thought she was going to be a running well of knowledge on the stand. I wanted her to discuss her baby daddy's antics, but she was unable to take the baton and run with it. Without the leading questions, my wife was, unfortunately, too nervous and ignorant of the law to inform the court of her situation.

Our attorney knew that he had been out smarted, as he was skillfully challenged by the opposing attorney. In contrast, our attorney did not prepare well for this caliber of courtroom exchange. It became obvious to everyone in the room that he was not ready for the twist and turns of his opposing council. The judge called the court to recess, as Rachel and I confronted our attorney.

My wife yelled to our attorney, "What the hell are you doing?"

I said to Rachel, "Baby, you have to give more passion and describe what happened when he asks you an open question. You have to fill in the blanks. You can't depend on him to lead you to the answer. The court is depending on you to provide a history, facts and depth to support your testimony."

My wife responded, "I am trying to provide the information that our attorney has instructed, so that I don't come off wrong or angry."

Our attorney said, "You're doing all right, but you have to fully answer the questions, by describing the entire ordeal of what you've been through. This is your story, and I can't lead you to the facts. I know we haven't gone over all the details, but you know your life and only you can tell the court what's going on with it."

The lunch break ended, and my wife was back on the witness stand.

This time, the opposing attorney began her cross examination by asking my wife: "Mrs. Sand, have you kept up with the joint-custody court order between you and my client, since 2005?"

"Yes, I have," my wife replied.

The opposing attorney continued, "Do you know if you have ever called my client silly, stupid or said anything that could be harmful if heard in front of your child?"

My wife replied, "No. I have not called him names in front of my son. I don't call him names, and I'm not aware of anytime where I have done that before."

The opposing attorney continued, "Mrs. Sand, where was your son on his birthday last year, in 2008?"

My wife looked toward the ceiling and tried to formulate her thoughts as she replied, "He was in Tennessee with me and my husband for that weekend."

The opposing attorney persisted, "Mrs. Sand, are you aware that on even years your child is supposed to be with my client, according to the court order of 2005?"

My wife replied, "I didn't keep up with all the details, as I should have. I simply made a mistake."

"Mrs. Sand, you said that you never violated the court order that was given in 2005. However, it is obvious to the court that you violated the order because you took the child on my client's birthday weekend!"

My wife was stunned for a second, and the court could clearly see that she was caught in a lie. She had broken the order. The opposing attorney, again, revisited the previous question.

"Did you ever call my client names or harmful things that your child could be influenced by?"

"No. I do not recall that."

The opposing attorney then said, "Your honor, we have clear evidence to the contrary that shows that Mrs. Sand is not telling the truth about keeping up her end of the order. She has also called my client names and lied about taking the child out of state, against my client's time and consent, against the court order of 2005."

Our attorney engaged, "I object to the admission of the tapes as evidence because they were not disclosed during discovery and should not be allowed to be submitted as evidence, your honor!"

The opposing attorney rebutted, "Your honor, we have provided a letter of discovery to the counselor's office, during the last three weeks since the last trial date that the new discovery period began. Mrs. Sand's attorney did not follow through on that letter to see what we had as evidence during this discovery period from March 27 to April 19, 2009. Mrs. Sand's attorney did not contact our office nor did he respond to our letter. Here is a copy of the letter dated April 8, 2009. It provides plenty of time for counsel to review our evidence, which he never bothered to do. Nonetheless, the opportunity and letter was disclosed to Mrs. Sand's attorney."

The judge asked, "Counsel, why didn't you follow up on this letter that was provided to you on discovery from the opposing counsel, in good faith?"

Our attorney answered, "I did not have the time or chance to follow up on the letter, your honor."

I could clearly see that our attorney was out of his element. He became extremely nervous and very frustrated.

He finally shouted, "Your honor, we do not know if this was a set up on my client or maliciously intended to smear my client as this was obtained by means that we can not prove. Your honor, the tapes should not be allowed to be heard in this case!"

The Judge stated, "Counsel, you had the right to examine this evidence by a letter given to you in good faith by the opposing counsel. You did not follow up on the tapes or inquire in the new discovery period before trial began; therefore, I can not keep the tapes from being heard."

This would be the climactic twist that would, ultimately, dismantle our attorney's defense. My wife's credibility was morbidly damaged, as the pendulum of the case began to swing in favor of the baby daddy. The first tape played a recording from the baby daddy's laptop. My wife was clearly angry and agitated on the tape.

Her voice resonated throughout the court, "You better bring my damn child back to me! I can't believe that you are trying to keep me from talking to my damn child! Where is he? Why is my child with someone else right now? God damn it! You better give me my child, you dumb motherfucker! You ain't shit, but a dumbass nigger! You just a silly-ass motherfucker! I'll call the police on your stupid ass! You'll be arrested if you don't give me my child! Let me talk to my child god damn it! You better not have my child around some other bitch, either! Please don't let me find that out again!"

The next tape played my wife's voice, in a calm fashion. "Hey, Mark had a death in the family. He lived in Tennessee, and we're going to a funeral this weekend. I am taking my son with me, and I know this is his birthday weekend. I hope we can exchange weekends when I get back, thanks."

Although this voicemail was left on the baby daddy's cell phone, the problem was that my wife lied about that birthday weekend to take the child out of state. Her son told his father that he went to a birthday party and had a great time. This was also proof that my wife lied and broke the court order.

The judge looked surprised and said, "Wow, Mrs. Sand! Is that you on those tapes played in this courtroom?"

"Yes. It's me," My wife shamefully responded.

The judge replied, "Do you know that you have perjured yourself by your own testimony in this court room today?"

My wife replied, "I don't remember saying all of those things. My child's father provokes me at times. He has a very controlling and conniving nature."

The judge stated, "Well, we should take a recess. After this, I have to get a relative from the airport. I thought that we'd be finished by now, but I will be back at 2:00 today. I don't do this all the time, but I have no choice today."

Recess was enacted and we were emotionally devastated with our attorney. The attorney looked like a deer caught in the headlights. He was clearly defeated, and I could also see that he was as disappointed, as I was with Rachel.

I asked, "How did you not know about the tapes, and what are you doing to help our case right now? What's happening and why are we in this position, at this point of this trial?"

I looked at my wife and asked, "Why did you lie? You didn't have to lie! You should have told the truth! You know you said those things to your baby daddy, and it was flat out wrong to deny it. You should have done the right thing, whether the attorney had a tape or not!"

My wife argued, "I lied, so that the court couldn't use the sour relationship with my baby daddy against me. It was embarrassing for anyone to know how we argued all the time. I did not want anyone

76

controlling my life, Mark."

I replied sharply, "You know you're under oath—you can't lie like that! Now you've lost all credibility. You could even possibly go to jail! Perjury is a criminal offense because you took an oath to tell the truth! He's a nobody anyway. You never had to argue with your baby daddy in the first place. You simply should have told him you were going to be with your husband that birthday weekend and let that be the end of the story."

It was 2:00 pm when court resumed, and my wife was back on the witness stand.

The opposing attorney was concluding her questioning of my wife when she asked, "Mrs. Sand, what will you do if the court does not allow your son to go to live in Tennessee with you and Dr. Sand?"

My wife sat back, sighed and replied, "Well, my son is my whole world, and it will be devastating for me if he is not allowed to leave. If he can't leave with me, then I will just have to stay here and take care of my child."

The opposing attorney said, "No further questions for this witness, your honor."

The judge then said, "Mrs. Sand, you can step down."

The judge took a 5-minute break.

In the meantime, I caught up with my wife in the hallway and asked her, "Were you telling the truth on the stand about staying here to take care of your son? You told me sometime ago that you would come home with me to Tennessee, if the court ruled for your son to remain in North Carolina." I reluctantly continued. "Baby, did you lie to me? Are you planning on staying here, if your son can't leave?"

My wife looked me in my eyes and said, "I will be in Tennessee with you, if my son can't leave the state," She continued. "I was answering the question the way the lawyer instructed, that's all."

I replied, "Baby, are you sure that we'll have a life together, if your son can't leave North Carolina?"

My wife looked at me and said, "Yes, I will be with you in Tennessee, if he is not allowed to come."

At this point, the baby daddy took the stand and placed his hand on the bible and swore to tell the truth under oath. Our representing attorney conducted the first cross examination. Our attorney had already seemed psychologically defeated, as he seemed to ramble with his questioning.

The baby daddy answered our attorney's questions, as if he had nothing to lose. He was confident that he had already hit a homerun out of the courtroom.

At one point, our attorney even stated, "You seem to be evading my questions like you know that I am running out of time here."

The time was 4:15 p.m., and the court trial period ended at 5:00 p.m., sharp.

At 4:35, the judge said, "All right, well counsel, it does not seem that you are going to finish cross examining the witness until next time."

My heart sank, as I began to sense that the judge knew that our attorney had already been defeated—it was truly sad.

The bailiff said, "Your honor, when would you like to set the next trial date? Will there also be a rendering of a verdict?"

The judge answered, "Make it as soon as possible, because the child will have to register for school soon. We need to get this settled and soon."

The court secretary said, "We have June 19 available and opened."

As the judge rose from her bench, she stated, "No, I know we can find a date sooner than that. We should really get this case over with."

I could not bear to hear the date and the continued nightmare of my consistent mental anguish. I got up and walked out of the court room frustrated and feeling like the probability of losing this case was high. I heard that the trial date was set for June 2, 2009. That was two weeks away, but it felt more like two months. I felt the control of the baby daddy and it sickened me, but I could do nothing about it. At the end of the trial day, I was furious at both our attorney and my wife.

The baby daddy shook my hand and said, "Mark, I hope no matter how this comes out, we can still be cordial with each other. You are a good man, and I want you to know that I respect you."

I replied, "Yeah man, whatever."

Inside; however, I felt as if he knew that he had already won the case and the trial.   It felt as if he was rubbing 'the victory' in my face, and there was nothing I could do about it.

I caught up to my attorney and interrogated him out of frustration.

"How could you let my wife put her foot in her fucking mouth like that? What the hell happened in there and why did you let it happen?"

Our attorney seemed so frustrated and ultimately defeated in himself that he said,

"I know it is a major blow in our case that dramatically weakens us, but we do not know how the judge will rule at this point."

I angrily interjected, "Why didn't you know about those tapes and why does it seem that you are not in control of the situation right now?"

"I am sorry. I did not expect them to have a rebuttal like that. Again, I am sorry for that."

I replied, "My wife could lose her child and what happens then? We are paying you good money and you are losing our case right now!

If we lose, we can appeal and try the case with another judge—but only if it comes to that. I don't want you all to be in that frame of mind right now. It was a hard day, but the judge seems ready to render her verdict. Right now, we can only pray for a positive result. I am sorry for today, I truly am."

As our attorney crossed the street at the intersection, my wife, her mother and I crossed at the opposite intersection. I could tell that she was crying and her mother was trying to console her. I felt mad, numb, angry and helpless because this was a situation that was out of my hands, and I could not fix it. The worst fear for a man is, usually, another man who manhandles your woman abusively or rapes her and leaves her scared, vulnerable and helpless. This is how I felt. The baby daddy used the law to make me a witness of a legal, mental rape, with a paid ring-side seat.

Life, from this point on, was nonexistent. It seemed to me that all the familiar things were now blurred. My wife and I did not feel good about the trial, and it was silently evident that this court case had taken a serious nose dive.

I finally had to say, "That was so dumb of you to lie in court!"

Rachel responded with tears and shouting, "I was trying to do my best!"

I told her, "Don't you know lying on the stand has put us in jeopardy!"

My wife simply said, "I am going to pray and just hope that everything will work out. I hope it will be all right."

The tears just poured from her eyes, and I had the sickest feeling because I knew that her credibility had been permanently damaged. All we could do, at that point, was pray.

June 2nd finally came, and I flew out of the Memphis International Airport at about 12:57 p.m. I wanted to catch the verdict of the court. I still had my surgical scrubs on from the office, as I did not have time to even change clothes. The flight was only an hour and fifteen minutes but we live in different time zones. Unfortunately, when I landed, the trial had come to an end, at 3:32 p.m. Rachel's aunt picked me up at the airport. Suddenly, she received a phone call it was my wife telling her that we would meet at her house to talk about the verdict. I was nervous and anxious to hear what the judge said. As we arrived at the aunt's house, my wife looked like she had been crying. I knew that was not a good sign.

Pulling my heart out of my stomach, I asked my wife, "What happened—what's the final word?"

She replied, "Give me a minute. I have to talk to my aunt for a second about something."

I was furious and replied, "I have flown here, trying to be supportive and going through this shit! You can, at least, put me first, so that I can know what the verdict was. I'm the one that has to live with it, not your aunt!"

My wife went with her aunt anyway, without even talking to me first. I felt abandoned.

So I just sat there, feeling like "Why did I even come here?"

After almost an hour, my wife came out and said, "Are you ready to go?"

80

I looked at my wife and said, "I have flown here to be with you and you still can't talk to me first, your husband, about something this important?"

My wife's reply was, "We can talk in the car on our way home."

I was angry as hell and all my support for her turned into frustration because, once again, I wanted to be first and let her know I was there for her, but for some reason, she could never put me first. I never realized it, until I wanted to console her and be her everything. Nonetheless, my wife seemed to have all those bases covered by family, her aunt specifically. Rachel finally told me in the car about how the court verdict went and how upset she was about it.

My wife said, "The judge ruled against me because of those tape recordings. The judge said that the tapes provided proof of how I violated the order and also when I perjured myself."

After retrieving the court transcripts, I later read the following verdict:

The judge stated, "In the case of Mrs. Sand versus the plaintiff, the court rules that Mrs. Sand has been proven by evidence presented to the court has violated the order rendered in 2005 by the court of Mecklenburg County and the state of North Carolina. It has been shown and demonstrated that Mrs. Sand violated court order section 16.b of the court order, subsection 9a rendered in 2005."

The judge continued, "Mrs. Sand, the tapes have shown the court that you are not honest with details to the father about the welfare of the child and has proven that your credibility, here in this court, was also not credible by an act of perjury against your testimony. It leaves me no choice but to sustain the current order from 2005 to continue permanent joint custody if you remain in the state of North Carolina. If you leave the state to be with your husband and have your unborn child, then you will relinquish full custody to the child's biological father, in which the child will remain a resident of the state of North Carolina." The plaintiff's attorney has included upon my approval that you shall have two weekends a month, with one weekend visit in Charlotte, N.C., where the child will reside, and the other

weekend where the child may go to Tennessee for that visit. You will be granted three, non-consecutive weeks in the summer as defined by Sunday to Sunday. Furthermore, in the months of June, July and August, the mother can have the child for one week in each of the summer months, but visits will stop 7 days prior to school resuming in the fall."

The judge concluded, "This is the order of the court based on the evidence that has been presented. You may appeal my decision but this is my ruling with the evidence presented in this case."

The bailiff stated, "All rise. All parties may leave the court room at this time."

When my wife told me this, I did not want to believe it. It really drove a stake in my heart, and I felt totally wronged by the system. However, I did remember that my wife told me that she would be with me, if her son could not leave the state. I held on to that statement now, harder than ever, because I really wanted to save our marriage.

Unfortunately, I would soon come to the conclusion that my wife could not allow her son to go to her baby daddy, and she could not trust that I would make a family around her son if she left him. I am sure it would be hard for any mother to do, but it had to be that way or lose our marriage, according to the court order. To see your wife having to choose between her child and her husband and their unborn child would be nothing less than devastating, to say the least. I could hear the crying of my spouse, as she wailed and cried from her soul. It was painful for me to see her go through this ordeal. Eventually, she would have to make a decision and do it where she could transition herself toward either leaving her son in North Carolina and sustaining her marriage, or staying with her son and basically becoming another baby mother all over again. I cried as well, and I can't lie—I truly did. After all, I am human.

It is very painful when the one you love is in misery, due to a selfish, controlling man, who just happens to be the baby daddy. The source of my wife's pain was unequivocally attributed to her baby daddy, who held her hostage, with the love of her child and made life miserable. I was amazed to see just how far a controlling man would go when it came down to court cost and living arrangements and all the pain and anguish that would affect everyone involved. It reminds me of the way that the bible tells us to do all things in our lives.

For example, I understand why we are supposed to wait before we have children and abstain from premature sex. I see now that by following these instructions, no man or woman can trap a person into a situation like the one my wife and I endured. In comparison to the old saying, "If I can't have her, then no one will." This is not only obvious for men who want to control women with a child, but this can also be applied to women who may attempt to control a man with a child. Either way, it always comes out sad and wrong as two left shoes. No one can be controlled, unless you give over your mind and will to the controller. In all cases, it is never good to allow someone else to control your life with money, children, a house and/or sexual orientation. It will never work because your true love will always come up short in life. Eventually, they may end up leaving you for less drama and more security. It is always better to be on the side of mature, well thought-out life plans, than to fall in to the calamity of control and deceit.

Advisedly, this is strictly my life's opinion and story unfolded for all to evaluate and learn from. Nonetheless, I urge each reader to place themselves in my shoes and challenge yourselves on what you would do, if you loved your spouse who proved to be under the control of a baby daddy, by love for her child. I am almost certain that most would have to agree that they would not even deal with that situation, in the first place. However, there are those who would take the chance in life and follow both love and their marital vows. Some would not wish for their unborn child to be born out of wed lock, if possible. In fact, if the husband and wife were willing to reconcile the marriage and make all things work, could it be done? The biggest problem, of course, is the derogatory effect on the children. They are innocent, yet, unfortunately, they are the key that is turned and played on by the controller who wants to imprison the counterpart who is interested in moving on with their lives. This could possibly work, but a few ground rules would have to be established.

First of all, if you were the parent giving up custody, you

would have to fully disclose your love for them because it is essential that your child knows that you are not throwing them or giving them away, in these unfortunate child custody circumstances. Secondly, set a scheduled time on weekends, birthdays and holidays to ensure that you will see them on a regular basis. This is so they will also look forward to the maintenance of the mother or father in their lives and never feel abandoned by either parent. Ultimately, the child will become stabilized in this living arrangement and not be tossed to and from each parent in a game of tug-of-war. This always leads to domestic failures and long-term psychological scars for the child. Thirdly, most mothers and fathers have to feel secure that the child will be safe and cared for to even make a decision of this caliber. I can not lie; it is probably the most agonizing decision any mother or father would have to make. In contrast, one would have to analyze the love and support of the spouse. This is because if you fail to free yourself from the control of past mistakes, then you can never be a wife or husband to anyone. You can only be a prisoner to your child and/or baby daddy or baby mother. Think of how inconsiderate this is to the spouse and/or significant other. If the rules are engaged and executed properly, the living arrangement should prove successful.

It had been almost twenty-two days since the court's verdict. She had recently stopped crying and began to gain strength. I could tell that she still worried about how she would deal with allowing her son to live with his daddy, while simultaneously holding on to her marriage with me. I knew my wife was extremely stressed and frustrated with her heart-wrenching decision. Throughout this time, I provided my support and assured her that she could actually be strong. She knew that I loved her and wanted a full life. Besides, I had a child on the way now, and I did not want my child to grow up without me, the same way I grew up without my father.

I did not like my wife's situation, but I loved her dearly. I began to call her, from time-to-time, and ask her for dates. Although time seemed to move very slowly for reaching a conclusion to be in Tennessee with me, I knew that I could not wait forever.

At times, I found myself literally begging my wife to come home.

She would begin to cry and say, "I will be there with you

Mark, I will. I just need a little time. My son will be devastated if he is not allowed to be with me."

My wife continued, "I want you to see your child develop in my womb and experience the pregnancy that is your first child. I want my marriage too. I just want my son with me, but I know it's hard because he is unable to leave the state. I know this is something that I will have to get used to, and I know in time it is for the best. This is so hard for me please understand."

I replied, "Rachel, I do understand fully, baby. I am here for you and all I want you to do is trust that I will make a good life around a living arrangement with your son and for our unborn child. I know your son will be with his father in North Carolina, and we will be in Tennessee. This will be for the best for all of us, so we do not have to be invaded legally by his tactics of holding you complacent, as a result of your son."

I was a little upset at my wife because she would never confirm a date with me. This really pissed me off royally because I felt that she was not being honest. She avoided taking the action of allowing her son to go to her baby daddy.

One day I called my wife, and I asked her, "Have you tried to negotiate some terms with your baby daddy?"

She replied, "No, I have not tried that, but we have not been on speaking terms for sometime now."

I told her that she should just try to call him and maybe we can negotiate something. I assured her that this could possibly be the only way to get her son. Rachel agreed and decided to open up lines of communication. She called her baby daddy. He told her that he was not pointing fingers anymore and was willing to negotiate for some terms of finding a resolution for their son to live with her.

I was excited and he basically asked that I come and help with the negotiations because he felt it was better for us all to talk things out. I felt that there may be some way to reach some form of an outcome. I know my wife was very happy with that possibility. I phoned my wife's baby daddy and we spoke briefly on the phone.

The baby daddy started the conversation by saying, "Mark, I want you to know that I am not a bad guy, and I did not think that the court order would have come out the way that it did. I just wished that we could have worked out something from the beginning."

I replied, "Well I think that is nice for you to say, and I hope that we can come to terms with a solution."

The baby daddy continued, "Mark, there are no winners with this current order, and I know that I do not want to repeat what I lived with having my father remove me from my mother at a young age."

I replied, "We just have to think as fathers now through this very situation. I know you do not want to hurt your son's heart by removing him from his mother like that. I know the court made a decision that affects our lives. However, it is up to us to make life work and reach some form of middle ground, and I feel that we can do that."

The baby daddy followed up by saying, "Mark, I did not know that you had some kids already?"

"I have one on the way, and I have to keep that in mind as I think about maintaining a marriage and family that I would like to come together soon."

"I just wish that we could have sat down some time ago, before we had to go through all of this. I know it is not your fault but at the time, Rachel and I did not get along as well as we should have."

I replied, "I know, but we can rise above the past and make everything work out for all of us," I continued. "I can fly down on June 28, that Sunday, if you want to meet to see if we can work something out."

The baby daddy said, "I feel that we should be able to find a way to work things out."

I thanked him and said, "I am sure that we can find a good way to negotiate and make all our lives work, in the best interest of the child."

I called Rachel. She was excited to hear that God was changing the heart of her baby daddy and giving her a second chance at life, by allowing her to take the child out of state. I was also happy, and I finally felt that we had a chance to be together as a family. My wife and I had to go to the baby daddy now because he had the court order and control of where their child went, due to his being awarded permanent joint custody. I felt that we had an opportunity to reach a positive outcome. Naturally, I also held a reserve feeling that after the baby daddy spent almost $17,500 to have control, it would not be that easy to get custody of Rachel's son. I was hoping that my gut feeling would be wrong, but this uneasiness continued to pull my mind. I guess this was my self-defense mechanism, just in case the deal went wrong. Eventually, my feelings of optimism were tucked away, so that we could proceed with negotiations.

I can not explain how it feels to go to a card game of life and have no "ace in the hole" or even a wild card to play. You feel vulnerable, as if you have no control of your destiny. You are basically at another person's mercy. The baby daddy could work with us or say, "Kiss my ass," and that would be the end of that. I did not like the odds, and the fact that I was a husband, married and dedicated to a woman, for three years, who had now become a victim of circumstance. This was the ultimate act of frustration; to literally have to go and beg a baby daddy, so that his child could come to live with us.

I began to feel silly and even wanted to back out of this no-win situation. Nonetheless, I knew that in my heart of hearts, I had to do all that I could do, knowing all that I had done, to see myself clear of this mess. I felt as if I had been sucked into a vortex. As I remained helpless and could do nothing, I truthfully blamed Rachel for getting us into this. Her past was, unfortunately, attached to my marriage. I could hear this in her voice and her weaning hopes and prayer. Above all, I just wanted her to be happy. I would have faced Satan himself for this. Most of all, I knew that I was on the losing end of a battle—facing a man who knew how to play on Rachel's fear and control her mind.

It is depressing to have your life's dream in arm's reach, with the reality looming overhead that you are utterly hopeless in aiding your own situation. Although, I was grateful to have a negotiating day with the baby daddy for my wife's sake; deep inside, I was not confident that he would allow his son to leave the state of North Carolina with us.

The day finally came, and I paid $693.00 for a plane ticket to Charlotte, on June 27, 2009. It was a Saturday, and I felt a level of excitement from my wife. I knew she was excited because she cooked some baked chicken, greens and rice with gravy and brown and serve rolls. If you knew my wife when she cooks, it is usually a sign that she is excited about something or feeling positive about the future. I really wanted to be strong for her. I finally wanted to see her happy, despite everything she had endured. However, I could feel that something was aloof. I tried not to show any emotions to my wife, but I did not trust the baby daddy to do right thing. After winning the court order in his favor, why would he give us the keys to our happiness?

In the end, I felt that Rachel lied to me because she could never find it in her heart to grant her baby daddy full custody. I would find myself losing again to the control of a baby daddy, over my wife, as he used the custody fight to intrude on my marriage. This control was very powerful, and my wife would be the only one capable of breaking this spell. This took an extreme toll on our marriage, especially since blood proved to be thicker than a marriage license. At least, this was my logic. Perhaps I was being selfish, but I could not fathom the idea of putting anything and/or anyone before Rachel. It was obvious that she did not share my sentiment.

8

The Joseph Syndrome: Getting away from the unexpected

It is really burdening to be in a position that you can not correct. This is especially true when you find yourself between the mess of two individuals who have placed themselves in a train wreck. It is repeatedly what I kept in my mind, as we began to get dressed that Sunday morning in preparation to meet with the baby daddy at Shoney's restaurant in Charlotte. We were about 5 minutes late, and I could tell that Rachel was nervous. I was open for anything at this point. I had drafted a proposal to present to the baby daddy to negotiate some terms that would be good for everyone. I even left opportunities for room to modify the proposal that I had written.

The proposal was very fair and straight forward. First, I would provide travel for the child, and I was voluntarily arranging for one weekend a month. Second, I was also proposing to provide summer travel and would even provide some special holiday travel arrangements like father's day and the 4th of July. I figured that providing a proposal to let the baby daddy know that he would not have to pay for the child's travel would have been a good thing. I thought it would not compromise the time frame of his visitation. The baby daddy and Rachel would meet at a public location to exchange their son.

Many outcomes came to mind as we drove into the Shoney's restaurant parking lot, and I could tell that Rachel was hoping for a good outcome from our effort. We entered into the Shoney's restaurant and informed the waitress that we were here to meet a party who had already arrived. Rachel and I walked to the back of the restaurant and saw both the baby daddy and his girlfriend. I was not expecting to see a female companion at the table. The baby daddy's girlfriend was his best friend. She was an African-American female with nappy-braided hair. This young lady also wore fake contact lenses, typically just a "Shenaynay," sister-girl look-a-like. It seems that she was once in the military, according to how she described her travel experiences. As we sat at the table and began to eat from the buffet, we discussed our plans. I could immediately tell that the baby daddy was not willing to negotiate a positive resolution, as he had previously alluded to on the phone.

Our conversation began by me saying, "Well, first I do want to thank you all for coming out and attempting to find some middle-ground on how we can all benefit from this arrangement. Rachel and I wanted to propose some issues to you, regarding the travel of your son.

I continued, "I will provide all travel for your child to get from here to Memphis, TN. Additionally, I will provide all summer travel as well. If acceptable, I will also provide for one weekend a month to adhere to the court-ordered visitation schedule."

The baby daddy replied, "Well, Mark, I think that is a great proposal, but how does that benefit me?" The baby daddy continued. "Mark, I really gave this a lot of thought since the last time we spoke, especially since recently returning from a Florida trip, with my son. We had a great time, and now I can't just see myself visiting with him. I really want him to stay here and be a part of my life."

I replied, "I thought you wanted to negotiate a resolution, in a way that the child could stay with his mother, as we spoke about on the phone?"

The baby daddy sat back and sighed.

He leaned forward and replied, "I am not trying to be funny, but I love my son. I know ya'll are married, but I love my son, and I want to see him every week and raise him here. There is nothing that you guys can do up there that I can't do here."

I replied, "Man, I know you are not saying that you are not willing to let this child go with his mother. I know you do not have any issues with me, so what's the problem?"

The baby daddy replied, "I just want to have my son here, so I can watch him grow up. I want him to grow up with my family and be involved in my life. I want to spend as much time with him as possible."

I replied, "We were looking to enroll him into a private school and give him a chance to have a great future. This school graduates students that go to Harvard, Yale, Columbia, Morehouse, Howard University, etc," I continued. "I am trying to give him a good life, while not compromising his relationship with you. I would like for his mother and I to very much be a part of this."

The baby daddy sat up and said, "Mark, that is good, but I want to send him to private school here," He continued. "Mark, I may not have gone to Harvard or any Ivy League school, and I may not be a doctor like you, but I am not hurting financially at all."

The girlfriend interrupted, "Well, Mark, I just want to say that Charlotte has some great schools, and he can get a good education here as well."

I looked at her and said, "I am here to negotiate with him. I cannot believe that I flew all the way here, and you are not even willing to negotiate."

The baby daddy said, "Mark, you and Rachel have not given me one scenario of the child remaining here with me, with you all visiting," The baby daddy continued. "What if I let the child go and your marriage fails? Then what?"

I was furious at the arrogance of this guy. He took a potentially peaceful resolve and created an aura of hostility by questioning the stability of my marriage. This was humiliating. He had never been married. More importantly, he had never even tried to step up to the plate and provide a stable relationship for his own child. I knew then the possibility of having the child leave the state was not going to happen. It was as if the baby daddy knew he had the order and the power to just toy with me and my wife. He wanted to make us grovel to imprison my wife's heart and hold my marriage hostage.

I replied, "Well, you do not have to worry about my marriage. My wife and I have been through quite a bit. As a result of that, we are here to stay and nothing is going to destroy us, not even this foolishness."

The baby daddy replied sharply, "You know I do not even have to be here talking to you, my lawyer told me that I do not have to do anything. In fact, if I just wanted to walk out right now and said the child goes nowhere, then that would be the situation and you all would have nothing!"

At this point it became almost impossible to hide the heated frustration from my face. As my wife began to cry, I watched the baby daddy smirk. It was almost as if his gratification level reached full throttle, right in front of my face. His arrogance led him to believe that he was running the show. I also couldn't help but to feel somewhat trapped myself, because I could not legally do anything.

After wiping her face, my wife interjected, "I am a good mother to our son. Why are you doing this? I thought that you were going to negotiate for a positive outcome," Rachel continued. "I have been a mother to our son since he was born, and I should have him with me. I have cared and done everything for him."

The baby daddy's girlfriend passed a napkin to Rachel, so that she could wipe her eyes. Rachel's lips were shaking, and I could see that she was becoming a nervous wreck.

I told my wife, "Baby, don't cry. We'll be all right. Don't give this guy the satisfaction that he wants right now."

I then said to the baby daddy, "You have the order from the court, but you don't have anything else."

He sat back and said, "Mark, this does not even concern you at all. This is between me and Rachel—about our son. In the end, I want my son here and not there."

I replied out of frustration, "You mean that you cannot find some form of common ground, so the child is not just ripped away from his mother, like you were by your father?"

The baby daddy replied, "My daddy stepped in when my mother was not ready to be a mother! He took me and raised me."

My wife responded, "Well, I am a good mother and no one can say that I am not a good mother to my child!"

Tears were streaming from her eyes, and I could see that this was going nowhere. I said, "What can we do to find a resolution? This is why I am here. What are we going to do about this situation? Are you telling me that we can not find some resolution that would work for everyone?"

The baby daddy said, "The only way I will even consider letting him go is that I get to spend some time raising him here with me. I want to watch him grow up, and I won't miss that. I propose that we do three years here and three years there. We can switch up every three years."

I replied, "Well, I do not see how that will work, but that is up to Rachel."

I asked Rachel, "How do you feel about this arrangement?"

Rachel looked dazed, and I could see that this was getting to be too much for her.

She replied, "I do not see how that would work. It seems like too much back and forth for our son," Rachel continued. "Well if I was to consider that, then let the first three years be with me."

The baby daddy replied, "Why should you get the first three years? I am only agreeing if I get the first three years."

Rachel responded out of frustration, "Our son is still quite small, and he needs his mother at these critical years right now. He needs to be with me, as I do everything for him and you know it!"

The baby daddy sat back and said, "I was only going to agree, if I got the first three years. So it doesn't seem like it is going to work for me either. We obviously can't seem to agree on anything today!"

At that moment, I wished for a gun. I probably would have shot that motherfucka dead, as he had to die. He was truly enjoying Rachel's most unstable moments, by using her son's love against her. He then presented a document about a house that Rachel signed when they were a couple, some years ago. It was a property in Myrtle Beach, South Carolina. He asked her to relinquish her rights to the property.

Rachel, being desperate for her son, signed her rights over to him. She then said, "I don't do anything with that property anyways, and I haven't been down there in years."

I suddenly found out why the nappy-headed girlfriend was present. As soon as   Rachel signed the property over to the baby daddy, the girlfriend took out her notary stamp and stamped the document. It seems that this was just a business transaction to clear up old business, but not for finding a positive resolution for the child to leave the state.

I was mad as hell. I just wanted to walk out right then and there, but I had to stabilize Rachel, as she was emotionally shaken. I could tell the baby daddy had control of her mind. She was so screwed up over her child that she didn't know if she was coming or going.

The baby daddy said, "Man, that food is getting to me, and I am starting to get sleepy now. I have to get ready and get off to church now."

I replied, "But what about all the things we are supposed to talk about today?"

The baby daddy replied, "Well, I am not doing or agreeing to anything without talking it over with my lawyer and right now, we do not have anything to agree on." The baby daddy continued, "Mark, it is a start, but you are looking for a one-day solution to this whole thing, and that's not going to happen. I know you want Rachel to move with you, but, right now, I am not satisfied with letting my son go and not be able to raise him partially. Mark, you do not have to fly down next time, we can just probably work something out over the phone or something," He continued. "I will probably call you guys by next week, Tuesday or Wednesday, or I could change my mind at any time. You never know."

I looked him straight in his eyes and I said, "I thought you were a nice guy, as you come off as some want-to-be-good professional, high-class Black male. You're nothing, at all. You can never be who I am, never!" Rachel and I gathered our things and headed for the car. Although she was a wreck, I was mad as hell. I knew that my feelings were right, and he simply wanted to clown and humiliate us since the court order seemed to be in his favor. For Rachel, this was her last chance to leave the state with her son, and I could tell she was devastated by the baby daddy and his foolishness.

All I could think to ask was, "Rachel, when are we going to move in together as a family?"

Rachel was crying and wailing on our way home. She knew she had a real crisis on her hands. I was full of frustration, at this point, and I wanted an answer after all that I had been through. Not to mention I had already been waiting three years on a marriage that seemed to never exist. I looked at Rachel, as tears kept streaming from her eyes. I could hear her crying more deeply with every breath, and it seemed like someone was taking her soul out of her body.

I asked Rachel, "Baby, I know this is hard for you, but can you please give me a date to make arrangements, so that we can keep our marriage and family intact. Please let me know something."

Rachel did not respond, it was almost like she was in another world, and I knew my marriage, for whatever the one that we had, was on the rocks. This was because Rachel was not going to leave her child with her baby daddy. I guess the baby daddy knew my wife better than I did. I thought about their past history of intimacy, and their shared lifestyle and living together for some years. In contrast, after three years of separate living arrangements, my wife and I had never lived together, not even for over a week. I know he will never release her child because the baby daddy wants to watch Rachel suffer. As antagonistic and sadistic as it sounds, remember that some people are just wired that way.

I knew that Rachel was having a difficult time with the thought of allowing a baby daddy to raise her child, as any mother would. I was aware of the horrible position that Rachel was in, but I also knew that if she remained here, it would indefinitely cripple our marriage and unfortunately compromise the life of our unborn child. Our current situation too closely mimicked the lifestyle that I was born into, and I could not fathom my absence from my child's life. My child would be automatically born with a strong discrepancy, without me as the father. The statistics on situations of this caliber are very prudent. Almost 54% of all African-American children in this country are without their fathers.

All of this ran through my mind, as I began to beg and plead with Rachel: "Rachel, can you please give me a date or a weekend time to come and pack you up and help you to move to Tennessee? I am here for you, and I have dedicated three years of marriage to you," I continued. "Rachel, your baby daddy is trying to use his own son against you by trapping you with your love for him. This is destroying our lives, and he knows what he is doing. Your baby daddy enjoys watching you suffer and being broken as a woman."

As we drove into the driveway of Rachel's house, I could see that she had a heavy heart. She was crying consistently, as she was very distraught over our last conversation with her baby daddy. The reality of what was happening with her son was psychologically crippling to her.

Rachel replied, "He might just change his mind by Tuesday or Wednesday. Mark, like he said, I can only hope for that. I feel like such a failure."

I replied to Rachel by saying, "Yes, you may have failed and made some pretty crazy decisions, but you can also change those decisions and straighten out your life. Don't allow your baby daddy and your past mistakes with him to destroy our life and our marriage. That's what will happen if you allow him to control you!"

Rachel slumped back into her depression, as she began crying again.

She replied, "I was thinking that I may be able to just allow him to go to his daddy and just try to disconnect myself from the pain of not seeing him everyday. It is the hardest decision that I have ever made in my life, and I feel like I need more time to make it. I love my son, and I just can't bear to see him go yet!"

Rachel fell on her knees, and I could hear her wail and cry. I was standing right next to her, but at that moment I did not mean a thing to her—only her son and her baby daddy were the priority. I felt like an outsider, as the life of my unborn child hung in the balance.

I shouted, "I am right here, Rachel! I am here for you. I have paid for lawyers and plane tickets for over three years. I have even tried to negotiate with your baby daddy today, by flying here. Do you see where all this has gotten us?" I continued. "I am really trying to reach out to you and make our life work, but your baby daddy has the court order and will not allow the child to leave with you. We do not have to lose out on a good marriage because your baby daddy is holding your son in this state for his own selfish reasons!"

Rachel then did something that I never thought I would see my wife do. She reached for a bottle of pills from her drawer and put them into her hands. She tried to cram the tablets into her mouth.

I sharply yelled, "Rachel! What the fuck...?" "I know you depressed, but damn! I know you ain't gone let this sorry muthafucka kill you and our baby! Hell, if you do this shit, he'll get your son anyway!"

I was frustrated with Rachel that she would allow herself to fall this low because of her baby daddy's control. She attempted suicide with 200mg of Motrin. Rachel had put at least 10 of them in her hand and was attempting to swallow them. I worked with all my might to stop her from taking those pills. As she was unsuccessful, I knew, at that moment, that our marriage was over and that my life with Rachel, as her husband, had been stolen right in front of my face.

It was the worst reality of a marriage gone wrong. I grabbed all of the pills, put them in a bottle, and put the bottle in my pocket.

I said to Rachel out of frustration, "I can't believe that you would let your baby daddy win like this and drive you to an all-time low!" I continued. "I can not believe that you would attempt suicide, right here in front of my face, Rachel. Killing yourself won't solve anything. Your baby daddy will still get your son. Remember, he is the biological father! Rachel, by committing such a selfish act, you would also be killing our child. If you kill my child, then I could never forgive you! Can't you see? This is exactly what your baby daddy wants you to do? He wants to destroy you, and he does not want to see you happy, married or anything else. He wants you depressed and in anguish, much like you are right now!"

Rachel replied, "I do not want to hurt our baby Mark, and I do not want to kill myself. I know you are right, but I am in so much pain right now that it hurts me to know that I am the cause of all this! I have let everybody down, including my son!"

I replied, "Rachel, you can conquer this and come home with me. We can still make a life for your son, and we will ensure that we build a family around him. We will see him as often as possible, and I promise you that he will always have a place in our family. Just trust me. We can do this!" I continued, "If we can not make this work, then we would have given our marriage over to this punk-ass baby daddy. C'mon, this is ridiculous, Rachel!"

Rachel slumped over her bed, in the master bedroom, full of sorrow and lifeless.

I pleaded to Rachel: "If you allow your baby daddy to control your life to this extent, where you don't want to live anymore or be my wife and have a life with me, then what marriage do we have anyway?"

I took off my wedding ring and placed it on the dresser out of disgust. Rachel was mentally drained, as the baby daddy had pushed her so far into depression, over her son, that she could not see our marriage or our unborn child. As I was right there in her presence, she was not even able to recognize me.

I said to Rachel, "What kind of marriage do we have when your own husband can not even make a life with you?"

Rachel remained silent. She was simply staring into emptiness as the room began to darken, while it was daylight outside.

I shouted to Rachel out of frustration, "Take me to the airport! I need to go home! I see now that I don't have a future with you. You have allowed your baby daddy to defeat our marriage and control your mind. This shit is truly sad!"

Rachel began to cry again and replied, "Mark, please put your ring back on! I don't want to lose you!"

"Look at you Rachel! You've already lost me. It seems that we are losing our future too!" I continued. "What marriage do I have with you when you cannot give me a date for our future? You're in hell right now, and I'm caught up in this baby mama versus baby daddy bullshit that should've been resolved before we got married!" I continued to speak out of anger: "It's not fair that I continue to suffer from all of your past indiscretions. They are killing our marriage and making my life a living hell—I deserve better than this!"

Rachel cried out, "Mark, please! I'm sorry! I want our life so badly that it hurts to be disappointed like this. I am going to be with you in Tennessee, I just can't tell you anything right now!"

"I can't believe you, Rachel! I mean, after three years of dedication and marriage, flying all these years to see you, accepting your child and paying for lawyers and being disappointed through thick and thin. You mean to tell me—your husband—that you don't know when we can have a real marriage because of some baby daddy's got damn child?"

I picked up my bags and proceeded downstairs. I put my suitcase in the car. Simply put, I was done. I had taken all that I could take and fought as hard as I could to save our marriage. I had just finished saving Rachel from hurting herself and our unborn child. She was confused and psychologically trapped.

When you really love someone, the last thing you want to see is that person hurting, even if you are not the cause of the pain. At this point, her son looked worried, and his eyes were glued on us as we all walked toward the car, heading toward the airport. I looked at Rachel as she possessed the look of someone who had been awake all night. The wife and friend I thought I could count on were gone. What was left, was a person that I no longer recognized. My marriage had failed. I began to realize that I would have to do something to find happiness. Unfortunately, the baby daddy was right—he held the cards to our future, through his control of Rachel. Although he was invasive and arrogant, I couldn't help but remember his words. I can see how true the baby daddy's power was over Rachel, even over our three years marriage.

As we began to drive toward Greensboro, N.C., to the Airport, I began to ask Rachel, "Why is it that you can't give me a date to be my wife and come home with me? Everyone else has a date to continue their lives? Why not us?"

Rachel continued her dazed expression and replied, "I will give you a date, but I can't give you one right now. I will let you know something later."

"Rachel, when will you let me know? I want a real marriage, so we can move on from this. Why are we having all of this confusion and stress between us?"

Rachel did not respond and kept driving. I was highly frustrated to the point that my patience was just about gone.

I asked again, "Rachel, your baby daddy is controlling this marriage and he is controlling your life. Why is our marriage failing? Is that what you want to see happen after you drop me off at the airport?"

Rachel replied, "No, Mark, I do not want my marriage to fail and the baby daddy is not controlling anything. He does not have me, you do! I am not being controlled by him. I just have a terrible burden on me, and I need a little time to deal with it!"

I replied, "If that is the case Rachel, then why can't I help? You deal with the burden and make plans for us to have a life through this mess. It has overshadowed our marriage all this time."

Rachel replied, "I will be able to be with you, but I can't give you any details right now."

"So, you are telling me that I have to wait around for you to figure out if we will have a marriage, when you and your baby daddy decide that we can finally move on with our lives. Am I not supposed to have any input, as your husband, or say so over my own marriage?"

Rachel replied, "I never said that, and you're putting words in my mouth, Mark!"

"If I am putting in my own words, then why are we now living according to what the baby daddy has already told me to my face? Why does he control our lives by having his child with you?"

Rachel did not respond. I could see that she had a hard time facing this critical question, because it hit her to the very core of all the confusion and stress that she was dealing with. All I could hear was the car on the road, while in the car was the deafening sound of emptiness. I had a bad feeling about the way Rachel was beginning to unravel. She began to cry silently, and I felt bad because I knew that deeply within, my wife did not want me to leave, especially without my wedding ring. However, I had seen enough destruction of my marriage by another man, for the rest of my life. I felt terrible that Rachel had put herself in this bad position of having to choose her husband or her child. No woman could win in that situation, and I felt terrible about it. I had witnessed how it made Rachel cry and get emotionally riveted.

Finally, we arrived at the airport in Greensboro, N.C. I looked at her son in the back seat and then I looked at Rachel and asked, "Rachel, he's an innocent kid, but he's here from a bad relationship. This situation is a prison from a pseudo man who couldn't give a damn about any of us or his child. Is it worth losing our marriage over this? Is it worth denying me from my child who was conceived out of love and a marriage?"

Rachel said no words and cried more frequently. She held up my wedding ring to me, and I saw how it affected her. I could not take the sight of how my heart was bleeding, so I slammed the car door, left the ring and grabbed my belongings. As I went through the automatic doors of the airport, it felt weird, but simultaneously I felt like a weight was lifted off my chest. I felt a small pain in my chest that began to go away as I checked in at the airport. My hands were actually shaking, but my grip on my bags was so tight that it left an imprint on my index finger that almost broke the skin. I did not feel it, until I dropped the bags and felt the pain in my hand.

I did not feel bad now and, somehow, I actually felt free from the marriage that I so desperately wanted to keep. It's funny how a travesty of some situations can bring out a side of you that no one can understand. All I could do in the airport was just look empty and catch myself starring into nothing, nothing at all. That was a real shock to me because I knew I still cared for Rachel inside, but her situation had right then made my life a living hell on earth. I finally felt free of the humiliation and stress of a bad situation. I don't care how strong a person is, when it comes down to the grind of a desolated marriage, it is then that the heart goes on survival mode. It needs to be free, from bullshit, in order to survive.

While in the airport, I ate a few bites of some food and tried to relax. I enjoyed not thinking about my situation for once. I enjoyed the freedom of being able to leave and go home to Tennessee.

When the airline attendant said, "We are ready to board for Memphis, Tennessee..."

I felt that God still loved me and was ready to free me from the state of pain I had felt in my heart that evening. It was the best flight that I had in a long time. This was probably because the flight was symbolic of escaping a bad situation, and I did not have to be reminded of a tragedy that seemingly unraveled in my face, over a bad, three-year marriage.

I remember how light the clouds seemed. It was about 6:40 p.m., and it was beginning to become dusk on the horizon. This beautiful sunset was just off to the left of the plane, yet I could see everything right from my window. I continued to watch the sun set and took on the rationale that it represented God's way of restoring me and closing the door on a long and agonizing day. As always, I began to pray for God to allow the plane to fly without trouble and to land safely. I also prayed that I could bare this pain in my heart. The pain I felt from the loss of my marriage and unfortunately missing out on the experience of raising my unborn child. I knew that Rachel would not leave her son with his baby daddy. How could she at this point? I thought about everything. I knew that in my heart of hearts, I truly loved Rachel. I knew that letting the marriage go would allow her to focus on life with her son, while allowing me to move forward. I figured I would let Rachel move on, as I did not want to see her cry anymore and continue dealing with this torment. I did not want to be a reason for Rachel's pain anymore, and the only way out of something like this was to cut my losses and leave.

I asked God for help. I mentally prepared myself to become a baby daddy. This made me angry because I never thought that after waiting 35 years to get married that it would lead me to this.

As the plane flew flawlessly into the setting sun, I began to ask myself, "How did I get in to this mess?"

Did I miss something that I could have foreseen? I tried to think of any warning signs that I may have overlooked. One, of course, came to mind. I thought of what my mother told me some years ago, before I met Rachel. Ironically, I did not think much of it until now.

She once said, "Son, if a woman is not free from her past and has a man paying child support, that woman is bound to that man by his child."

I prayed for God to give me the strength to move on from that moment. I remember hearing how, sometimes, baby daddies and mamas can spoil a relationship, on the Michael Baisden Show. All-in-all, I never thought I would actually become a victim. Who knew?

I had a sense of what may lie ahead, so I began to think to myself about life and what it meant to me. I philosophized on where I went wrong. I felt like I had been let out of prison. I was optimistic and elated about life's possibilities. I recalled that I wanted to reward myself with a trip to Saint Martin, in the Caribbean Islands. I simply love the Country of Saint Martin and its people. They have the greatest sea food. I love the lobster and fruit smoothies, and the red snapper is wonderful. The beautiful people of Saint Martin are dear to my heart and have provided great comfort to me through their atmosphere of white, sandy beaches. They are heavenly with tropical sky blue water. It is simply a magical place to the eyes, especially when one has seen nothing but frustration and pain. The blue water and the bright sunshine is a perfect camouflage to shed some tears off the lovely balcony at the Holland House Hotel in Phillipsburg, a town on the Dutch side of Saint Martin. Saint Martin is an Island inhabited by two countries, the French and the Dutch. I enjoy the friendly people who know how to party. I am always welcomed there, and I love the people. The Black people like me are very approachable. The fusion of nationalities, cultures and languages are simply beautiful to observe. I felt a part of the island whenever I visited. This was my getaway from the day-to-day and, let's not forget, my crazy marital problems.

I felt right at home to see how the lovely people of Saint Martin supported President Obama. It was extraordinary to see the locals display their pride when hanging President Obama's photo in their businesses and homes. I also enjoyed staying at the Divi Little Bay resort. This beautiful hideaway is located in Phillipsburg, a major resort locale, on the Dutch side of Saint Martin. I would simply say to all men who need a pick-me-up, take a quick, three-hour plane ride to get away from a boring day-to-day existence. St Martin is where you need to be. The friendliness, pampering and service you get from a different country makes you feel like a real man again. Don't forget about the massages. I get mine from the therapist at the Divi Little bay resort. They are wonderful at relieving your stress. Their fruit smoothies are to die for, and the sea food is nothing like anywhere I have tasted on earth.

Saint Martin has friendly beaches and social clubs, with relaxing lounges. The music is great and the people are very friendly—there's hardly any crime. I enjoy the beautiful atmosphere, and I am always blessed to be in the presence of the friends that I have made. I traveled to Dominica. This is also an island in the Caribbean. In my travels, I have made some great friends there too.

Last year, I was actually in Dominica for the country's 30th International Independence Celebration, with my dear friend, Sigmund, and his family. I went to a wonderful place called Screws. It is a natural, warm sulfur spring oasis that one must experience to fully digest the concept. It is absolutely beautiful, with huge pools of natural sulfur, spring warm water, at various temperatures to your likeness. There are beautiful, lush, green-leafy palm trees that align the pools to drape the wood hand railings that guide you down the stone path to the sulfur pools. It is very enchanting. Some say it has healing powers that help many people with aches and pains.

I observed many lovers in the pools as they did something strange and wonderful. The couples do not move, yet they hold each other very close in an open, reclining fetal position, with the female in front of the male. They then allow the sulfur streams to roll over and between their bodies, while submerged shoulder deep in the pool. I am not saying they were intimate under the sulfur-gray colored water, but they looked very satisfied with each other, so that they did not move much—just enough to stay in that position (you figure that one out). The beautiful people of Dominica really know how to party, and I needed a good party.

The Dominican locals partied all night, even until the sun came up in the downtown stadium surrounded by palm trees and mountains. I was so tired, but I truly enjoyed myself. This trip gave me an opportunity to get what happened to me and Rachel off my mind. The sweet Caribbean music was great, and the smell of grilled chicken and fresh fried fish and chips filled the air. The lovely red snapper fish dishes with grilled chicken and daushin, a vegetable similar to potatoes, was very good.

From Dominica, I returned home and became restless in Memphis, Tennessee again, because no matter where I went, I would often think about Rachel and how she was doing. I did not want to reach out because I was still upset about how the whole situation seemingly ruined my life. Therefore, I set out to travel again. This time, I stayed stateside and went to sin city. That's right—Las Vegas.

I know that many say that it is sin city, but Vegas has always been a great place to go to get wild and have a good time. I love to check out some of the cool shows. I went to see Oscar and Grammy-winning recording artist, Jamie Fox. He had a good show. His song "Blame it" was great, and everyone got up and got their "groove on." Say what you want, but Vegas is still a nice getaway if you want to do something different. I walked all over and hit a couple clubs and even managed to catch the Lion King show—it was really good! I was so amused and impressed with the whole musical arrangement. I had a chance to catch a conference in Las Vegas for my professional surgical training. While there, I had the opportunity to meet some new female colleagues of various professions that showed me a great time. I enjoyed myself immensely in their company. It was nice to get away from the house, phone calls and stress that had built up my life. I wanted to be away for awhile. I learned when a man is hurt and wounded he will travel to the ends of the earth to get relief. This happens so that he can feel his manhood again, to find his place, through his pain. The people that I met on the "heal my heart tour" did my soul good.

Ironically, I found myself praying a lot. Praying is a way that many African-Americans release stress and allow God to do what he does best—heal our pain. I know that most people will say, "You did not do anything to deserve what happened to you." However, I find that with prayer and releasing things, that I can turn control over to God. This allows me to get old gracefully, and I would rather age slowly than rush it with all sorts of stress and anxiety. In the end, you can't do anything about it anyway.

I did not call Rachel at all, as she did not call me. I was really feeling like I could not talk to anyone but my close colleagues like: Dr. Mangle and Dr. Handie, my most trusted friend, Dr. McIntyre and my good friend Dexter. I do have one other person that I have found great to talk with—my mother. I try to keep family affairs out of my marriage. This is so I will not taint my mother's perception of Rachel. To talk to her is a real treat from time-to-time. I can appreciate her honesty and experience with love.

Once I thought about Rachel and what this whole situation did to her. I felt that we were at a great stand still. I was tired of being alone and feeling devastated. I made up my mind, after all this time, to file for divorce and just let Rachel go. Not out of anger or spite, but out of love for her. This was because I knew she was in a horrible situation. To ask or even pressure someone to leave their child to salvage a marriage, how can you rationally do that and be happy with yourself?

Eventually, I knew what that was going to mean for both me and my child. I cried for, at least, half the afternoon, even while on my way to the attorney's office. Rachel was about three and half months pregnant and not really showing much, but you could tell that she was pregnant if you looked close enough. I was really hurting and wondered if I should go through with this. Nonetheless, I knew that if I did nothing, then nothing would ever happen.

As Rachel resided in the state of North Carolina, with her first child and my unborn child, I had nothing to look forward to. I would not wish this situation on anyone. The sadness is too painful to relive—just writing about it. However, I am over that period of my life now, and I thank God for that. So I did get to the attorney's office as the office resembled a beautiful museum. It had white, tall columns and the justice bronze blind statute on the outside of the building. There was tall wrought-iron gate closures around the property, so I knew this had to be the place. As I drove into the gated area, parked and walked into the attorney's office, it was really nice with a very professional secretary.

She asked, "May I help you?"

I replied, "Yes, I am Dr. Sand. I am here to see Mr. Larry Wise."

The secretary replied, "Oh, yes of course, let me go and get him for you. Would you like some water or tea while you wait?"

"Yes certainly, I would like that."

I sat down and began to try to organize my case of papers when Mr. Larry Wise approached me and said, "Dr. Sand, how are you sir? I am Larry Wise, and I am going to have you come into the office. We'll hear just what has been going on with your life and assist you in doing something about it."

Due to confidentiality and privacy laws, I will not go into detail about our conversation, but I will tell you this: I felt he was the best divorce attorney that a client could have. Mr. Wise really listened well and he rarely spoke a word. He allowed me to express myself fully. I was so full of emotion that when I began to speak that I actually began to shed tears from the stress and heartbreak of the situation. I discussed everything in the first hour of our consultation. It was almost like having a front seat on a train ride to hell. Mr. Wise actually wrote a book about this very subject and the book is like a guide to the topic of marriage and divorce. It really serves as a tool for how divorces should work and the rights of the father and mother kind-of-thing. I was impressed by that. He had been married, himself, for over 30 years to the same woman that he met in high school. That solely impressed me. He seemed to be a great hunter, as there was a huge bear and a head of a bull stuffed in his office. His office yielded all sorts of pictures and beautiful outdoor fishing and game hunting that he was proud of. Every man needs a hobby and a release from the pressures of everyday life. It was refreshing to see that he had found his release and pleasure. I loved all the beautiful, dark cherry oak wood and artifacts that he had throughout his office. It was nicely arranged and beautiful. I noticed various newspaper clippings of his career achievements and goals. This made me feel more confident in talking with him about my marital crisis.

After about an hour of listening to me, Mr. Wise sat back in his executive office chair and said, "Dr. Sand, many guys come in and they tell me what they have done and they have really made a mess of things in their marriage. However, you actually did not do anything wrong. It seems that your wife simply lived her life and got herself stuck between a rock and a hard place with the law. More specifically, the previous order that was established before your marriage. Unfortunately, that is the real tragedy."

From that point on, I felt vindicated and actually shed a few more tears right then. This is because I knew that I did not do anything wrong, but I wanted someone of authority to vindicate me. This person was neutral and non-biased to my situation. What he said really made me feel that getting a divorce was not only a wise move, but it would be good to relieve myself from a bad circumstance that could have gotten uglier.

I hired Mr. Wise right then to be my attorney, and I just enjoyed his style of listening and not talking, until the full matter was heard. He then called his paralegal and told her to take down my situation. Mr. Wise sat back in his chair and just told everything to his paralegal, Mrs. Westwood, word-for-word. It was amazing because he did not miss a word of what I said. I was simply impressed at how much he took in, while I was speaking and shedding tears. He was paying me full attention and seemed to care for my story. He allowed me to tell everything, from my point of view, and I felt clean, free and thankful to God for that.

At that point, the stress left me, and I felt optimistic about everything. I had not told Rachel that I was going to file for divorce, and I am not sure I wanted to tell her right away because I had felt so much negative stress from our previous conversations. I wanted Mrs. Westwood, the paralegal, to talk to her. So Mrs. Westwood called and left Rachel a message. She then called her back to share the legal divorce proceedings with her. As many would think that this might be cruel to do, I was totally fed up with my pseudo-marriage. I knew that at this point, conversations about divorce would only add fuel to the fire, and I wanted to get away from stress, heartaches and separation—not aid it along. I felt that by calling her, myself, would have done just that.

My phone began to ring a day before Mrs. Westwood called Rachel to tell her about the divorce proceedings. It seemed that Rachel was trying to reach out for me, but I had already made up my mind. The next day, I happened to answer the phone, as Rachel had gotten the message from Mrs. Westwood that I was filing for divorce.

As she was livid about this, she screamed, "You mean, you are going to get a divorce from me, while I'm trying to hold on and get myself together, so that we can have a marriage? Why would you do that?"

I replied, "Rachel, Our marriage has been stalled for over a year now. With the court rulings, thousands of dollars spent and the frustration of talking to your scam ass baby daddy, I know there is no future for us," I continued. "I do not want to be in a marriage anymore where I have to travel over 500 miles, just to see or spend time with you. All of this because of some damn, baby-daddy court order. I didn't get married for this type of life!"

Rachel shouted, "I love you Mark! I really do and I know I messed up but please don't end the only thing that I still have! We can make this work!"

I was upset with her and yelled, "How the hell can you make a marriage work when the law has already ruined it and dictated the rules of the game to you? Your son is in North Carolina with his daddy. In order for you to be here with me, you have to ask for permission," I continued. "I love you too, but I do not want a marriage like this anymore. I know it's hard for you, but it's really hard for me because this means I can't see my baby grow up everyday. This is the real shame because I've never even seen a photo of my own dad. Now, here I am losing my child because of you. I actually hate that we have a child on the way, Rachel!"

I could hear Rachel beginning to cry again, and it was because all of her past guilt was crashing down on her. I could tell that she was feeling terrible at that moment. I felt bad because I loved Rachel but due to her bad situation, it was going to cause me to be a baby daddy when I got married to be a father.

I had waited 35 years to be married, and I did not have any

children before I got married. So, why was I looking forward to becoming a father and a good husband? I gladly took on Rachel's child because when I was a child, I always wished that some good man would have come along and picked me up to take me places and love my mom, my brothers and sisters, but that never happened for me. I figured I would take a chance and make that happen for Rachel's child. This situation really separated not only a marriage but a stable family. This was all because a man had paternal rights to a child. At this point, he had never gone to school programs or supported his child. The court had even scheduled the time for him to spend with his son. Quite frankly, he wanted his child to hurt Rachel and to ruin her marriage.

Rachel concluded, "I am coming up there, Mark. I am going to fly there and you need to pick me up from the airport."

I replied, "Rachel, that's not going to be a good idea. We don't have anything left to talk about. Besides, if your situation does not change, there's nothing anyways!"

I continued, "Rachel, the only person that is enjoying your suffering and watching you go through the motions of all this is your baby daddy. He can still watch his child grow up and pick him up at-will, now. In the mean time, he now can watch the control he has over you and watch everything you love begin to be taken away from you!"

Rachel replied, "Ain't no one in control of me! I'm in control of my life, and I don't care nothin' about that motherfucker...fuck him! I love you, Mark, and I always have. I'm not giving up on us...I want my marriage, and I'm coming up there. Do you hear me? I'm coming!"

"Rachel, I have already filed for divorce, and you are not supposed to be here. So, I don't want you to come here. You don't even have to call me anymore."

Rachel replied, "I am coming all the same. I know I messed up but that does not mean that I can't love you. I want to make things right, Mark!"

"Rachel, you'll have to sacrifice something, if you want a life with me. This is too painful for both of us. Unfortunately, at the end of the day, and after all of our yelling and screaming at each other, you know that you can not leave your child with his daddy in North Carolina!"

Rachel cried very hard for second and replied, "I want my marriage and I don't want to lose what we have."

I felt terrible and said, "Rachel, I am sorry for how you feel right now, but you know I can't do anything about it. As your attorney has told us, "…only you can change it."

I then said to Rachel, "Don't try to drive or come here, it will not change one thing, unless your situation changes. This is the only way that things will change for us. In the meantime, I want to be free of this horrible mess that you've gotten us in to!"

I hung up the phone and that was the last conversation I had with Rachel that day. I did not get anymore calls from Rachel that entire day. I was told by my attorney to limit phone conversations and allow counsel to handle all of the conversations, from this point on. I went home and stretched out—tired from a long day at the office. I was not feeling positive about Rachel. Honestly, I did not hate her. I was just numb. Consequently, outside of my horrible situation that brought about this stress, tension and grief, we really did have a nice relationship. I remember having the oddest feeling that night, as I began to get ready for bed. My friend, Dr. Mangle, called and we spoke briefly. He said that Rachel had tried to call his wife to find out if I had spoken to them about our situation. She wanted to know what I was thinking, about the divorce proceedings. Dr. Mangle shared his concern with me. I thanked him for that. Shortly thereafter, my mother called to inform me that Rachel had contacted her. Rachel wanted to know if she had spoken to me, since I was not answering my phone. My mother wanted to know what was going on. After Rachel shared the news with her, she was understandably upset with both of us.

She said to me, "You all are in a real mess here. But getting a divorce could be a good thing if that's what you really want. Don't be no fool! Do the right thing and pray about it. The Lord will tell you what to do, even in a bad situation, as long as you pray and ask God. He'll help you through this."

I thanked my mother and hung up. I thought about what Rachel's mother told me a few weeks back, after the last court ruling.

She said, "Mark, my daughter got caught up in a real spider's web, and she did it to herself. I'm ashamed at how she got herself into such a mess with that boy. But I told that girl not to go to court without a lawyer, the first time she went. Rachel didn't listen to me and messed herself up something terrible, for the rest of her life. Mark, I just wish you didn't have to go through this," She continued. "You seemed like you were so happy with everything on your wedding day. When I look at your picture, it made me smile. Your smile was so bright—I could tell you were in love. It's a hard place for a woman to be where Rachel is."

My Mother-in-law continued, "To be with your husband and raise your child, you have to leave your first child with the daddy in another state. If she keeps her first child, she'd become a baby mama, all over again, except she would have two kids and lose out on you. This is a real spider web, Mark. And if you ever do decide to get a divorce, then no one could blame you. You are still a young man, with a great career as a Doctor ahead of you. I know you won't have any problem finding you someone in a better situation, if y'all can't make this work. You will always be welcomed in my home, and always be looked at as my son. Mark, you have been a good man to my daughter, and I know you didn't ask for this—I wish I could take it back for you. I'm ashamed when I think about how my daughter is acting. It makes me sad to see how your marriage has broken down like this, but it's clearly not your fault. No one is accusing you of anything."

Rachel's mother really had a way of putting things into perspective. It was a real relief to hear how her own mother proclaimed me to be a good man to her daughter. She knew that I had simply tried to help her daughter as best I could. I humbly respected Rachel's mother as my own. As her mother is a Preacher and hard-working woman, she built her life around faith as did my mother. Furthermore, we both agreed that this marital dismantling was not my fault. I especially felt vindicated hearing it from both mine and Rachel's mother. These people respected me most and knew me as a person. They loved both Rachel and me equally.

With all this in my head, I got ready for bed and went to sleep. At about 2:43 a.m., I heard my door bell ring. I knew who it was. I have to admit that I was surprised to see Rachel.

She had put her face right up to the window, with tears in her eyes, and said, "Mark, I'm here, I'm here! I don't want to leave. I want my marriage. Mark, please!"

I opened the door to let her come in, as her son was with her too.

I replied, "Rachel, what are you doing? You know this child is not supposed to be here!"

I was surprised and excited but when I saw her son, I was furious because I knew that she made a hasty decision to come here. She did not have a choice because she had no babysitter, so she took the child and drove all day and night, just to talk to me. I must admit, that really showed me how much she cared for me, but I pondered her situation. Nothing would change, unless she changed it. Obviously, the situation had not changed because she had to go back to North Carolina or risk jail time and going back to court.

Rachel said, "Mark, I just wanted to talk to you face-to-face, so you can hear from me and know that I love you more than anyone in this world. I drove all day and night because I needed to know from my heart if there is anything left for us to hold onto. Mark, I am carrying our child. Look at my development. I want a marriage for our baby. I need you and this baby needs you too. Just hold me. Put your arms around us and know that I we love you, Mark."

I put my arms around her, and felt my baby inside of her. I thought to myself, that is my child, but my moment of glory was quickly shattered by the reality of hearing her son say, "Mama, I'm sleepy. I wanna lie down, but it's dark in the other room." Our embrace was cut short because his voice reminded me of why I could not have a life with Rachel.

I told her, "You come here with the baby daddy's child and try to get close to me? You know you're not right. This is the shit that led to this mess in the first place!" Rachel began to pick up our wedding picture, which I kept in the great room.

Mark, why do you keep this out if you do not want us to be together any more?"

I replied, "That photo is special to me and it reminds me of special times. We could have continued it, if you'd told the truth from the beginning."

Rachel tried pulling me into our master bedroom and said, "Mark, lets make love like we used to. Let's be a happy family again. I love you and I know we can make this work!"

I showed Rachel our king-sized master bed and bedroom. I explained, "For three years, I have been waiting for you to be my wife—to share this with you. You never took that serious enough to stay here. I'm tired of being alone and holding up this marriage. What's worse is that I'm still lonely whenever you're around. I still don't have a marriage, as long as your baby daddy has control. He controls you because you have to go back to North Carolina and make sure he gets his child, even though I suffer here alone. Isn't that right, Rachel?"

Rachel just cried and said nothing.

9

<u>How we survived a tragedy</u>

"So making love to you is all I have done for three years? Yes, we are blessed to have a child as a result but if we only make love and never make a marriage and a home together, then what do we really have, Rachel?" I continued, "This is not why I filed for divorce, not because I don't love you, but because we are not building a marriage—not now, or ever...since the beginning. The only person that has been enjoying life has been your baby daddy, and I will be damn if I continue another day under his rule!"

Rachel asked, "Mark, do you still love me?"

I replied, "No, Rachel...if it means I cannot be happy, have a real marriage and raise my unborn child then no. I can't love you like that, living under these circumstances. I'll always care for you and love my child, and I will take care of my child!" I continued, "Rachel, you cannot stay here. I am going to get you a hotel, where you can stay the night. There is a Best Western on Hwy 64. I'll pay for one night's stay."

I took Rachel and her child to the Best Western hotel where the bill came out to around $184.00.

I paid the bill in cash and then asked, "Rachel, do you need some money for food?"

Rachel said that she did not. I had about $75.00 on me, so I gave it to her. I walked her to the hotel elevators, and she hit the third floor button. The elevator door closed. I stood there for a moment, as I watched the number return back to the 1st floor.

As Rachel exited the elevators and walked toward me, I began to speak, "I wished that this would have never happened to us...I feel bad believe me, Rachel."

I looked at her in her green top. She was about 3 months pregnant, now. I saw in her eyes tears of sadness and defeat, and I got choked up. I began to cry, as I turned to walk away. As I got into my car, my phone rang...it was Rachel.

She stated, "Mark, I know you know that I care about you. You are the most special person in the world to me. I thank you for getting the hotel for me and the extra money tonight." Rachel continued, "I just want to say that I could feel how you looked at me. You wanted to reach out and hold me. I wanted you too. I just hope that you still have love for me, Mark. I want our marriage. I drove all the way from Charlotte, N.C. to Memphis, TN—551 miles just to say that to you. I know that meant something to you because it means something to me."

I replied, "Rachel, I've loved you, since we began dating. But love is not our problem. Your court orders and the invasiveness of your baby daddy in our marriage is the problem. Unfortunately, there's only one way to resolve it. Choosing this option will allow us to have a future here, together in Tennessee. I am not sure that you can make that sacrifice. Only you can decide to allow your child to live with his father in North Carolina. This will allow us to raise our child in Tennessee, without any interference in our marriage. I can't ask you to make that decision, only you can make it. It has to be from your heart, so you'll have to think it through. In the end, you'll have to be able to live with your decision." I continued, "Take some time and think about how much our marriage really means to you and what it would mean being a woman with two kids, from two different men, living in two different states. Look at things from this perspective: we are separated from each other and disappointed with how our marriage has dissolved. I am sure your child can feel the disappointment when he sees you crying at night. All of this has been over a simple court order that has dominated our marriage this past year. Do you really want another child born into this form of marriage based on what we have today? Does our child even deserve to have such a desolate family life, where the father is missing, and you are miles away? The child's life is torn, even before the baby has a chance to come into the world. Rachel, is that the marriage you really want? I hope not because I will not have that for myself or this child!"

Rachel said, "No, I do not want that for our child, and I do not want that for my first child. I do not want to continue having him torn between two parents or to be used by his father for some sort of power, over my life. I am sorry that this has ruined our marriage, but I will pray to God for direction in what to do about this. It is so hard to think about allowing my son to go to his father. I know he will not hurt him, but I have been his mother from birth. My child has always been with me, so to come to grips with this reality is too hard for me right now. I know what the court has decided, but they did not birth him into the world, and they did not nurse my child from an arm baby on up—I did!"

Rachel continued, "I know what I will have to do to be here with you and raise our child together. I'm just trying to come to grips with this Mark, Okay? I am trying to hold it all together right now, and it doesn't get any better with you getting a divorce from me. I know you want a divorce because of what has happened—I can understand. This mess is my fault! Mark, I'm sorry. I swear I'm sorry for everything you had to go through because of my not knowing. Mark, can you give me another chance? Even as you go through with this divorce, is there a chance?"

I replied, "Rachel, I love you, and if you can allow your child to go to his dad, according to the court order, and we reconcile by having you move here with me, then we can certainly start over. I promise you I will help you to heal, and I will work with you to see your child as often as the court order allows. I love you, and I want to make our marriage work, but I have to know that we can and must do this, according to the law, so that we are not invaded again from your past."

Rachel replied, "I will need some time and it will be hard, but I know I want my marriage and I want to be with you—I do not want to be alone with two babies." I listened to Rachel, and I could hear that she felt some hope over the phone. I told Rachel, "I have an early morning flight to catch to Nevada for a conference this weekend. We can talk sometime later, after this weekend."

I asked Rachel, "Are you sure you can let your son be with his dad? Can you be married to me and raise our child together, with your son visiting twice a month? I will make him feel just like a part of our family."

Rachel stated, "Honestly, I can say yes, for sure. It'll be hard, but I'll need some time to talk to my child. My heart tells me that this is the right thing to do, but my motherly instincts are ripping my soul apart, just thinking about it, Mark."

Rachel began to cry again, and I could hear how this was

bothering her deeply.

I stated, "Rachel, take all the time you need. I'm going forward with the divorce because even with all you know to be true, you still have to face yourself. Do what needs to be done, so you can be here with me, without regrets. On the other hand, I'm not sure that you can go through with this. I don't trust it; if I can't hear you say it with confidence. Whether you can or you can't, right now, our lives are hanging in the balance, while you're waiting to come to a conclusion." I continued. "Rachel, be safe driving home. Stay at the hotel and get some rest. You need to rest before getting on the road again. When you are really ready for a life with me and have made up your mind, please let me be the first to know. Our marriage has always been 2nd or 3rd, after your child and your baby daddy...This is what destroyed us, Rachel!"

Rachel replied, "I know I could have made better decisions in my life, and I am asking God to help me make better ones. Will you give me another chance to make a good life with you, once everything is right?"

I replied, "Rachel, I just want to be a good father, husband and physician. That's all I have ever asked God for. I want you to know that I trust you to do what is right but for now, you are still holding on against a court order that gives your baby daddy control. By remaining married, your baby daddy, unfortunately has control over the life of my child. I will not live like that and I won't ever fight you for custody like your baby daddy. I won't have a marriage where another man has authority because he has a kid with you. Take a few months to think about what you want. The divorce is final in October of this year and by then, if you decide to allow your child to go with his daddy, we can make time to sit down and seriously discuss our plans."

Rachel said, "Okay, I can do that. I'll take time to get myself together. I'll call you when I'm ready."

I replied, "Rachel, take your time. I am not in a rush, and I don't want you to decide anything that you can't live with. You have to remember that this decision will affect the rest of our lives, so pray and seek God. Consider some spiritual counseling and do some soul searching. Let's look at how we let a damn baby daddy, tear up our marriage. I'll wait to hear from you. I'd like to know something in the next few months because the baby's due in December. If possible, I'd like to know what's in store for us before then."

Rachel replied, "I can certainly respect your honesty, and I thank you for giving me some time to think about things. I need to know what I can live with...I need to know if I can make it without my son."

I was glad that I had spoken to Rachel, and I knew that she was happy too.

I completed our phone conversation by saying, "All right Rachel. I'll talk to you in a few weeks. Let's see where things go from there. Have a good rest and be safe driving home tomorrow."

A few weeks came and went, and Rachel called me from time to time to check in. As discussed, she actually spoke to a spiritual counselor at her church. Rachel even got baptized. Her pastor and his wife actually counseled her about our situation. They told her not to feel ashamed and that God ordained marriage. They instructed that our unborn child was not a mistake; rather, she was a miracle and deserved a mother and father who would love each other and the Lord. They expressed the need for us to raise our child in the fear of the Lord, together. They finally told her that by allowing her son to go to his father was nothing of which to be ashamed.

10
When a Miracle happens and life begins

The pastoral counselors allowed Rachel to see how the law had decided about the child, but not her motherhood, nor the possibilities of moving on and having a good life with her husband. The unborn child would need loving parents to deliver a balanced, spiritual guidance and would, together, love their child daily. The counselors taught Rachel that the problem with most marriages today was the outside influence of the world. When the grounds of a marriage are sacred, no man, woman or child can challenge its stability.

These great lessons taught by her counselors also complemented my sessions. Furthermore, I felt these spiritual lessons were just what we needed, in order to re-establish positive communication. I began thanking God that we were talking again, learning from Godly principles and developing a stronger level of communication. We learned to leave the past in the past, by refraining from negative words and thoughts that fed emotions and energies that worked to tear us apart. This book began from a series of journal entries that progressed into a non-stop passion. I literally watched God and time, through love and compromise; allow two people, at the point of complete grid lock, regain their ability to communicate. Our progress was slow, but this was a good place to start.

I remember watching the Black in America 2 series on CNN. This was an inspiring study on various African-American lifestyles, from economics to the Physician. There was even a segment on marital challenges, among African Americans. I truly thought this piece to be inspiring. I thought Soledad O'Brien did a fantastic job on demonstrating the divorce rate for African-Americans. She highlighted it to be very high—around 73%. I could relate to the reality because it was happening to me and Rachel. Sadly, we had become a part of the statistic. The show aired a couple who discussed how they struggled with communication issues. I clearly saw Rachel and myself dealing with the very same things. The gentleman stated that he would not leave his wife because he knew that she had his

119

back, regardless of the situation. This is why they boasted a successful and lengthy marriage. The wife declared her husband to be an excellent father—good with their daughters. The show introduced a marital counselor named Nesa Muhammed. She was excellent with her methods.

I remember Nesa Muhammed saying, "You have to find a way back to the place in your marriage, where you are worth saving to your spouse. Communication is the key, and you have to put each other first. Hold that sacred from the world. If you have that as the foundation in your marriage, then you can always find a way to overcome any challenge to the marriage."

I really held on to that and was so impressed with the comment that I wrote it down, as a reminder. I was now at the point that if Rachel and I continued to get better in our communication, we could later return to a state of marital bliss. As our divorce was now final, the possibility of remarriage was on the horizon. This would allow us to break the curse of the past, plagued with bad decisions and the baby daddy from hell.

It was July 27th. We'd been a part for roughly half the year. She had come to a conclusion and wanted to discuss a few questions. Hopefully, my responses would suffice, at least, enough to allow her child to go with his father.

Rachel asked, "If I let my child go with his father will you promise to help me see him as often as possible?"

I replied, "Yes, I will—no problem. I will make him a part of our family. I promise."

Rachel felt good about that answer.

She then asked, "Mark, can you promise me that you are not going to walk out on me and our baby, if we get together again?"

I replied, "Rachel, your mistake was allowing a devious, scoundrel boy-of-a-man to impose on our marriage. He has been the cause of all this mess. I can promise you that I have never let anyone separate you from me, and no one will ever separate me from my child. This, I know for sure."

Rachel replied, "I know where I went wrong, and I'm confident that I will never put anyone or anything first, over you again. Be it children, people or anything else, you will always be first in my heart, I promise."

"Rachel, is your son with his father?"

"I have called him to make the necessary arrangements. School is getting ready to start, so I have made up my mind. He will go to live with his father. He seems more and more excited about this. I guess he's getting bigger now. Maybe there are some things that his dad needs to show him."

Rachel expressed what was truly in her heart. I listened and internalized what she was saying.

Rachel rationalized, "I know that his father is an asshole for what he's done, but I know that he loves his child. I'll trust in God that this is the right decision. I'll always be his mother, and I'll see him twice a month. We'll have summer weeks together. He understands that I love him and I'll always be there."

As I listened to Rachel, I could see how the counseling sessions had really helped both us. I could see how the positive messages of faith and trusting in God had really paid off. We had experienced a tragedy that drove us to divorce. All that we endured showed me the power of reconciliation and the separation from selfishness that had often clouded our vision from what was truly important.

Rachel continued, "Mark, I love you and over these several months I've realized that I'm not happy without you. I love my son, and I know he'll understand about my decision to be with you. My place is beside my husband. I'm ready to be the wife that you need, and I'm tired of being alone. I just look at the phone sometimes and wish that you'd call. I know we agreed to give each other time, but I want us back. We're divorced, but if you would have me, I am more than willing to try again. I promise you that I'll never let anything come between us again. I promise you, from the bottom of my heart, Mark. Baby, please believe what I'm saying to you."

I can't lie. After hearing Rachel pour her soul out to me, I could not help but to feel a revival of our love. My heart felt strong again. I missed her like crazy, and I was lonely too. Moreover, by Rachel allowing her son to live with his daddy showed that she was strong enough to move forward and make a life with me. We could finally have the marriage that we both wanted from the beginning. I was glad that she made the decision for herself. As I gave her room to think, we had both arrived at the realization that we missed each other tremendously.

I said, "Rachel, I have waited for you to come to this decision ever since we've been apart. We're ready for the future. I'm so happy with everything you've said. I can't even explain how happy I am, right now. We can raise our baby and have more children. Your son will be a part of our family—I promise you that. He will have a home with us, he'll have a foundation." I continued, "Rachel, we will need a prenuptial agreement. This isn't for me. It's iron-clad protection against your baby daddy. After coming with me, he could devastate our finances, my practice and the life I've built for us. It's obvious that we love each other and with the baby daddy gone, we can make a better future for ourselves."

Rachel replied, "Mark, I totally agree with you. I am so happy that we are able to look forward to the future again. I feel good talking to you. My stress is gone. I'll be home soon, and we can begin raising our baby. I went to the doctor's office today…we're having a girl! I hope you're happy. She is healthy and doing well."

"A girl! She'll be daddy's little girl. I couldn't be happier."

Rachel and I thanked God on the phone and discussed the healthy ultrasound that she had in July. It is absolutely astounding to witness how God brought us from where we were to where we are, right now.

I demanded, "Rachel, I need you to be in Memphis tomorrow. Can you come?"

Rachel responded, "Mark, what's going on?"

"Rachel, just be on the first flight to Memphis tomorrow morning, please!" "Okay, okay! I'll call you when I land."

The very next morning, my heart raced with anticipation as I broke every speed limit getting to the airport. Her flight was landing soon, and I wanted to be there as she came down the corridor. Damn it! I couldn't find a place to park. This moment was too important. I took a chance and left the car in the loading zone, with the hazard lights flashing. I ran full speed to the area where she would be walking toward. I counted the heads and faces with smiles of hope, until finally…there she was. Her hair bounced perfectly and her face was the most beautiful face I'd ever seen. Rachel dropped her bag a few feet in front of me, as we both ran toward each other. As we embraced, I remember thinking, "I've never held anyone tighter than this, in all of my life."

We must have kissed, in front of all of Memphis, and we didn't care.

We separated momentarily as Rachel attempted to speak, "Mark…"

"Shh," I immediately interrupted. I got down on one knee, in front of God and everybody. "Rachel, will you marry me? Say yes. I have the perfect place. Let's go to the bridge—our place. You know we have history there.

Rachel began to cry and fell in to Mark's arms.

She whispered, "Yes, I will marry you, Mark. I will be the wife that I always wanted to be for you."

Mark and Rachel held each other and kissed again, with renewed passion.

Rachel said, "Mark, I am so glad to be home with you, in Memphis. Wherever you are, my heart is happy and safe."

"We're home, Baby…finally. I love you now and I always will.

Afterthoughts

I hope you can make it to the release party. This should be a great story to remind people that God can restore even the worst marriages. If you divorce, that does not mean that your life is over. God can heal divorces by restoring communication, especially if you believe in love and trust your heart. Are you willing to put your spouse first? Faith in God and trusting in the love of one another can prevent you from becoming a divorce statistic. Rachel and I are happy after all we have been through. We are living together and planning the arrival of our beautiful daughter in December. We are extremely excited about our remarriage. In salute of this reunion, we are hosting a step in the name of love baby shower and ball. We are inviting all our friends, family and well wishers that have been praying for us.

I am thankful to announce the launching of my friend's new radio show—the Dr. John Bell Show on KWAM990. The show airs on Saturdays from 4 to 5pm, CST. The show starts on August 8th. It can also be heard online at KWAM990.com. I wish all readers of this book many blessings and may heaven smile upon you.

To the future generations, I add this pearl of wisdom: Always put your faith in God and heed to his guidance in your life. Always trust your inner voice of what you know is right, and you will rarely ever go wrong. Trust the voice of love and put nothing above it. Know that life will test that voice, but never allow your inner ear to lose its sound for wisdom. Furthermore, when challenges from outside of your marriage or relationship come at you, will you have a clear connection to love and a great wealth of knowledge to withstand the temptations of life? Above all my beloved, never let your faith fail for the love that all human beings are destined to find. For if you seek it with a clear, open and passionate heart, then you will most certainly find what you need in God's human creation. Thank you for reading my book, and I hope it helps someone to believe in love as love truly never fails and always covers a multitude of faults, even those that are not your own.

10 Pearls of wisdom if dating/marrying a woman or man with a child

1.) Always make sure the past has been correctly ended with no court orders that bind the baby daddy or baby mama to your daily dating or marital life.

2.) Make sure that you know all court orders up front to decide if you can live with a court-arranged lifestyle.

3.) Know what state laws govern your paternal and maternal rights.

4.) Make sure you know what you want out of a relationship and if you can handle a child.

5.) Be sure that the child of the woman or man you are dating can leave the state if your job relocates

6.) Make sure that the man or woman that you are marrying is not still married or separated

7.) **Note**: be sure to get a **prenuptial agreement** to protect your personal belongings in your marriage

8.) Make sure you know the personality of the child to see if this is a child that you will get along with in a family situation.

9.) Above all, if you are single with no kids, it is my humble advice that you try your best to meet a man or woman, who is also single with no kids. Ensure that they are available and ready to start a life with you. This is truly the optimal way to begin a marriage.

10.) Be honest. If a woman or man with a child is not what you want, don't try to have a one night stand because it is not worth hurting the woman or the man for some 15 minutes of sexual satisfaction. Furthermore, please do not hurt the innocent child by building a false relationship for sexual gratification. Trust me; it will always end in a painful and frustrating experience. Be true to yourself. Are you capable of the staying power required for real love? Do the woman or man with a child a favor. Save them and yourself some drama by walking on by. That man or woman is trying to make a family and, perhaps, rid themselves of the curse of the baby daddy or baby mama.

*Please visit our website
for more information at
www.drjohnbell.com.*

*You can also join Dr. Bell on facebook at
facebook.com/Dr.JohnBell.*

Notes

Notes